SERVED
Cold

A BEST REVENGE NOVEL

SERVED
Cold

A BEST REVENGE NOVEL

MARIE HARTE

Entangled Publishing, LLC
2614 South Timberline Road
Suite 109
Fort Collins, CO 80525
Visit our website at www.entangledpublishing.com.

Brazen is an imprint of Entangled Publishing, LLC. For more information on our titles, visit www.brazenbooks.com.

Edited by Noah Chinn
Cover design by Fiona Jayde
Cover art from iStock

Manufactured in the United States of America

First Edition September 2014
Rerelease November 2017

ENTANGLED
BRAZEN

Chapter One

"Ms. Weaver? Andrew keeps poking me."

"But he started it!" Andrew protested.

"Nuh uh. Josh saw you."

Josh confirmed Andrew had started it, as did a few other students.

Ann drew in a deep breath, counted to five, then slowly let it out. A glance at the clock showed another ten minutes until school let out for the week.

She gave the young troublemaker her stern face. "Andrew."

All it took was his name. He burst into tears and started stammering apologies. If only they were all so easy to manage. She broke apart two more squabbling seven-year-olds before returning to Andrew.

God, what a long week. I need a drink.

After calming him down, she restored order to the class. For once, it took little effort to get them to clean their desks before struggling into their jackets and backpacks.

"Ryan, put your jacket on." That one was always trying to sneak around in short sleeves, and with early October bringing a bite to the air, she knew his mother would appreciate him bundling up.

He smiled, showing a missing front tooth. "Yes, Ms. Weaver."

Once the scamp put on his jacket and got in line with the others, she checked the time and gave a sincere smile just as the bell rang. "Okay, guys. See you Monday."

With a cheer they left the room to their parents and bus lines, and Ann puttered around the room so she too could leave. The weekend couldn't have come at a better time. Though school had recently started, Halloween already loomed on the horizon. The kids had started chatting about costumes and candy, excited about the prospect of a parent-endorsed sugar rush.

Her phone buzzed and she read the message. She texted back a confirmation on wine night at Riley's. A professional baker, Riley always had the best goodies at her house. She was their go-to girl for gatherings since Maya could barely boil water, and Ann couldn't compete with Riley's prowess in the kitchen.

More than ready to head out, she left, talking to current and past students as she started her walk home. On her way, she saw Josh hanging out of the car waving madly. She knew he lived close by.

"Bye, Ms. Weaver!"

She smiled and waved back. Next to him she saw Laura Bloom, his grandmother, driving. Nice family…if one could forget about Jack Bloom. Even after all this time she hated to think of him, but having his nephew in class made it difficult to pretend he didn't exist.

She put him out of her thoughts, as she routinely did these

days, and finished her walk home in peace. After tidying up the small cottage she'd been lucky enough to purchase, she changed into comfy clothes and read a book, wishing she'd had the funds to accompany her parents on their two month tour of Europe. Must be nice to retire, she thought, imagining her mother's fascination with touring ancient castles and her father's annoyance at managing the conversion rate of the Euro.

A few hours later, she left for Riley's with a bottle of wine, a plate of cheese and crackers and a solid attitude. She didn't even have to knock before the door opened.

"What took you so long?" Riley frowned at her, then smiled seeing the wine. "Ah. The price of admission. Welcome." She took the food and wine from Ann's hands before Ann could offer them.

"I feel so used." Ann brushed past the chef of the Terrible Trio—what friends and family had labeled them back in elementary school—and found Maya sitting on the couch, already drinking. "Am I late?"

The frown on Maya's face didn't detract from her beauty. With rich coppery skin, dark hair, and dark eyes courtesy of her mother's Native American roots, she made Ann feel like a pale frump by comparison. The blah redhead with freckles and an odd penchant for tanning—her one saving grace considering most redheads burned.

"I had a hell of a day," Maya complained. "I mean, bad with a capital B."

"Don't ask." Riley closed and locked the front door before making a beeline to the kitchen. Already the smells of freshly-baked something made Ann's whole world better.

"So what happened?" Ann smirked when she heard Riley's muffled groan.

"I'll tell you what happened," said Maya. "Some creep decided he didn't like my prices on Etsy so he started two-starring my stuff. I mean, you don't like the work, fine. But to rate me low because I charge for shipping, like everyone else? Suck it, dickhead."

"Nice mouth," Riley yelled from the kitchen.

Ann turned. "Why are you yelling? You're like four steps away." In a house with an open floor-plan. Just as cute and tiny as Ann's place, Riley's had all the charm of a fairytale cottage. Wooden floors, creamy walls, comfy furniture. And that dream kitchen where good, sugary things came to life.

"I'm yelling because she gets hard of hearing when she's drunk."

"I'm not there yet," Maya protested. "Besides, I'm not drinking because I'm angry. I'm drinking because I'm *hungry*. Where the hell are my cookies?"

"Cookies and wine. Yum." The combination clearly indicated the trio's lack of sophistication. Just the way they liked it.

Ann settled beside Maya on the couch and watched Riley work. She looked more like a model than an actual baker, with cocoa skin, bright brown eyes, straight black hair pulled back into a ponytail, and a face that could have made millions in advertising.

Tonight, Ann felt uglier than usual around her friends. She sighed. "Geez, Riley. Do you ever sweat?"

"You want my bodily fluids in your food? Really?"

Maya grimaced. "Christ. I'm drinking here. Do you mind?"

Riley snorted. "Whatever. Just make sure you use a coaster."

"Yes, *Mein Fuhrer.*"

Riley flipped her off with a dough-covered finger.

Apparently done riling the cook, Maya tugged Ann to face her. "So, my day might have been bad, but yours is gonna get a whole lot worse. Get some wine in you."

Dreading the bad news Maya looked all too gleeful to share, Ann fetched herself a glass and sat back down. "Go ahead. Shoot."

"Drink first," Riley ordered from the kitchen. "You'll thank me later."

"So you know too?" Ann took a sip and eased into the couch. Better to be relaxed when getting hit by a mental two-by-four, in her opinion.

Maya blew out a heavy breath and announced, "Jack's back."

Ann faltered a moment, then took another sip. A big one. "Jack Bloom?" As if Ann cared about any other *jack*-off. She mentally high-fived herself for the pun.

Maya regarded her with concern. "You okay?"

"I teach his nephew. I expected to hear about him at some point from his family. I mean, Josh is in my class." She shrugged, trying to appear casual. "So he's back in town visiting?"

"Back in town to stay, or so the rumor mill is spinning." Maya finished off her wine, then started on the cheese plate.

"How do you eat so much and stay skinny?"

Maya shrugged. "Bad genes."

They chuckled. It was no secret Maya had issues with her long deceased mother. Old wounds took a long time to heal, a lot like Ann's emotional quagmire anytime she thought about Jack Bloom. "He's back."

"That's what I said." Maya watched her. "So?"

"So what?"

"So vent a little. Remind us all again what a stupid, lousy creep he was for breaking your tender heart at sixteen."

"Seventeen. And we've been through this too many times to count."

"Come on. He's a loser and a shithead for getting you pregnant and dumping you in the same breath. For choosing

Selena Thorpe of all people, a girl with breasts bigger than a pair of Goodyear Blimps." Maya was on a roll. "For taking back his ring when *he* had the nerve to—"

Riley cut in from the kitchen, "Let's be fair. Ann didn't even know she was pregnant before suddenly she wasn't. A blessing in disguise, I'm thinking. And it's not like he dumped her because he found out. He never knew."

Jack had never known about it, and she planned to keep it that way. A senior in high school planning to go to college, she hadn't even *thought* about having a child. That nature had decided she wasn't ready helped ease the grief she'd had over the incident. It still didn't seem quite real, as if the experience had happened to someone else long ago. A faint memory, a bittersweet relief.

"But he ruined you."

Ann frowned. "You know, Maya, you don't have to be so dramatic about everything."

"Yeah, right," Riley added. "Drama's her middle name."

"Fine. 'Ruined' might be harsh. But the way he dumped you for that bitch Selena was just wrong, any way you look at it." She held up her glass.

Ann clinked it with her own. "Well, that's true. But my cousin told me that Selena's on her third marriage, so karma's on a roll."

"I love karma." Maya smiled. "Still, you need to get prepared to face that jerk. And let's be honest. He might not have ruined you, but you sure don't trust guys the way you used to. Not enough to date for more than a few weeks before you dump them. That all goes back to Jack."

"Not true."

Riley joined them with a plate of cookies. "I have to agree with Maya on this one. Not all guys are selfish idiots with the compassion of radishes."

"Radishes?" Maya cocked her head.

"I'm in cooking mode. Gimme a break. Look, Ann, your parents are happy. And your dad is obviously a guy."

"No, really?"Ann deadpanned, but Riley talked over her.

"He can't be a total loser or your mom would have dumped him years ago, right?"

Maya agreed. "I love your dad. My dad's awesome, and Riley's was great too. I mean, he didn't kill her at birth and throw her back to the wolves, even though she was a scrawny, ugly thing. A lot like she is today."

Riley rolled her eyes. "Yes, I'm so thankful he didn't murder his own child because I'm so hideous." She'd lost him to cancer at a young age, but by all accounts Darius Hewitt had been an amazing man. "The *point*, Ann, is that you've let what Jack did mess you up when it comes to dating."

"Oh, and you're any better? How's your love life?"

Maya snickered. "Try nonexistent. Say what you want about me, but when I want sex, I get it."

"Sure you do, Miss Ass," Riley mocked.

"Jealous?"

"Please. This baby got back." Riley smiled and bit off the head of a sugar cookie man.

"You guys are terrible for my ego, you know that? After a week of dealing with hyperactive children, I'm told that I'm scared of men and made super-aware that I'm the only one of us that has no ass." Ann drank more wine.

"Ann, get real. You're petite and hot. All the guys are after you." Maya helped herself to a cookie and bit the man's legs off. "I love these."

"You're welcome." Riley turned back to Ann. "She's right. You could date, you just choose not to."

"I'm selective. That's not a bad trait." She pointedly glanced at Maya—the polar opposite of selective—who ignored her.

"So what's the plan?" Riley asked. "How are you going

to handle Jack?"

"I'll handle him just fine. Don't worry about me. But you? I saw Anson yesterday." A blunt effort to change the subject, and it worked.

Riley's eyes burned. "That hack? I thought he lived in Portland."

"Apparently he's back. Dexter's in town too." Dexter Black, Anson's cousin.

Maya choked on her cookie, then downed some more wine to clear her throat. "What's going on? Did hell freeze over?"

Ann smiled at the happy coincidence, no longer the only one under the gun. "It seems that fate has given us back our worst enemies. Time for some do-overs, ladies. I tell you what. I'll deal with Jack, and I won't be pleasant. Aren't you guys always telling me that I'm too nice?"

They nodded.

"Not this time. How about some payback on the golden boy for treating me like crap? If he has the audacity to even try talking to me, I'll make him wish he'd never come back."

"I'll believe that when I see it," Maya said.

"Oh, you'll see it. But you two have to stand up for yourselves too. Maya, you need to deal with the one boy who got the better of you. And, Riley, maybe you can finally put your rival in his place. What do you say?"

Talking about vengeance out loud had empowered Ann. Finally, she'd get Jack out of her mind and her dreams. Confront him head on, say what she'd been dreaming about saying for years, then leave him with his proverbial tail between his legs. Oh yeah, that totally had appeal.

Maya just stared at her.

"What?"

"Color me impressed. You sound a little mean, Ms. Weaver," she ended in a singsong voice, imitating any one of

Ann's students.

"Hey, you try to deal with twenty six- and seven-year-olds all day. It turns you nasty."

"If she can do it, I can for sure." Riley rubbed her hands together and gave an evil laugh. "Anson Black, you are *so* going down."

"No reneging," Maya warned. "We see this through. It'll make us all stronger in the end. Confronting fears, handling the past—"

"Eating more cookies," Ann recommended, and bit right into her cookie's nether region.

"Ouch." Riley laughed and held up her own headless sugar man. "A toast to us. And may revenge be as sweet as the icing on my cakes."

Chapter Two

Ann spent the remainder of her weekend running errands and seeing the latest thriller at the movies with her friends. She, Maya and Riley had been inseparable since the first grade, and she didn't see that changing any time soon. Through the boyfriends, the challenges, the wins and losses each had experienced, they'd been there for one another.

Now, they'd have their revenge.

She'd have hers sooner than later, it seemed, because Monday afternoon, who should arrive to pick up Josh from school? None other than Jack "The Ass" Bloom.

Her pulse raced and her whole body seemed to come alive. She could feel him looking at her through the classroom door while she pretended not to notice. She and a few mothers who'd been helping with a class project readied the kids to go home for the day.

"Ms. Weaver! Ms. Weaver! Uncle Jack is here."

She inwardly groaned but refused to turn and face his overwhelming presence until she was ready. "That's great, Josh. How nice for him to visit you at school."

"He's takin' care of me for a week. Mom and Dad are on business in San Diego."

Terrific. She'd have to see Jack before, during *and* after she gave him his verbal ass-whooping. Ann stood straighter. This had been a long time coming. No point in half measures.

Then again, with all the kids around, she'd probably have to delay their little talk. She had no intention of getting into anything with her students or their parents near. But if Jack tried to hang around...

The bell rang. She told Josh he could open the door, and the students filed out.

To her chagrin, the room emptied in no time and nobody came in, leaving her pumped up for a confrontation that didn't happen. Feeling let down, she grabbed her coat and shoulder bag and headed home. Her heart raced when she saw Josh sitting in a car in front of her house. The boy must have told his uncle where she lived since he passed it every day going home.

Be calm. Be cool. She slowed her pace and reached the car at the same time Jack got out. Good Lord. He'd gotten even better looking in the twelve years since she'd last seen him. Proof positive that life was not fair.

He still towered over her at more than six feet to her five-four. Short brown hair framed a handsome face, from which his bright blue eyes blazed. Had luck been on her side, he would have gotten slovenly and out of shape. Instead, he looked muscular even under jeans and a blue sweater.

"Well, well. When Josh told me Ms. Weaver was his teacher, I was hoping it was you."

To her shock, he enveloped her in a bear hug that took her off her feet.

Familiar warmth, desire, and a need to be closer caught her off guard. She hadn't expected him to be friendly—or that she'd be so receptive.

Before she could struggle to be put down, he set her back

on her feet. "Still as pretty as ever."

She felt as if she'd stepped into an episode of *The Twilight Zone*.

"You used to know Ms. Weaver?" Josh asked through the open car window.

Jack had the nerve to slide a finger down her nose. "Know? We used to date."

His teeth were so white and straight. She wanted to punch a hole through them. Instead, she forced a smile. "That was a long time ago. How are you, Jack? You look good." Amazing, to-die-for sexy, hotter than any man had a right to be. *Why did you just tell him he looked good, dumbass? This is not the time to be nice. Remember what you did to the sugar cookie.* Yet she didn't think she could take a bite out of his groin, even if Josh hadn't been staring at them.

"I'm good," Jack was saying. "I transferred from Washington to teach at the OSU satellite campus here. The school is transitioning to a four year program, you know."

"I read that." Great. No way he'd be jobless and move anytime soon. The state-funded project had been given the green light.

"Just the excuse I needed to come back home. I sure missed Bend." And her, by the way he seemed to stare at her. She recognized carnal hunger in that gaze.

What. The. Hell?

Twelve years ago, while he'd had an arm draped over Selena Thorpe's shoulders, he'd announced they were done. Just like that, in front of the entire cafeteria. No explanation. No concern about breaking her heart in two. She'd erupted into embarrassing tears, and he'd looked bored by it all. After a minute or two, he'd asked when she thought she might be done crying, then walked away laughing with Selena.

She'd been the pitiful laughingstock of the school for two solid weeks before Bethany James ran off with Carl Longtree and became the new talk of the town. Then things had gotten mostly back to normal. But not this normal.

As if reading her mind, Jack said, "The past should stay in the past, right?" He smiled. "We're old friends, aren't we?"

"Are we?"

He laughed and hugged her again, and she was torn between wanting to slap him and wanting to kiss him—which horrified her.

"Of course we are," he said as he let her go. "I think Josh might have told you, but I'm taking care of him until Dan and Julie get back. They're away on business." He caressed her cheek until she stepped back.

He sure had turned into Mr. Touchy-Feely. She wanted badly to tell him what she really thought, but with Josh hanging on their every word, she swallowed her wrath. For now.

"Nice seeing you, Josh."

"You too, Ms. Weaver."

She looked at Jack and let him see the frost in her eyes. His lips curled, and she gripped the strap of her bag with a tight fist. Punching him in the face would not set a good example for the little one waiting for his uncle. "Jack." She nodded and stepped around him and his expensive car, then walked up the steps to her porch and let herself in the house.

She shut the door behind her and slumped against it, shaking from the confusing mix of rage and desire coursing through her. Tears pricked at the backs of her eyes, the need to go back to a happy past conflicting with the pain she still felt, even after all these years.

l. But she couldn't convince herself not to care. *It'll go away as soon as I get some ass-kicking closure with Jack Bloom.*

Now that she believed.

· · ·

Jack drove Josh home, only half-listening to his nephew

prattle on about a game he'd played at school. Ann fucking Weaver. *Of course* she had to look like the delicate fairy princess he remembered. But she was older, wiser, and damn, even hotter now.

She still had that same blood-red hair. *Wine-red*, she'd always corrected him. So deep and rich, and it still curled around her shoulders in waves. Ann seemed just the same as she had in high school, though her body had filled out in all the right places. Despite her petite size, she had really nice breasts. Which fit in his hands perfectly, if he recalled.

Man. Talk about fate kicking him in the teeth. Back in town for only two days and he'd run into the one woman he'd never been able to completely get over. Even when dating other women over the years, something would always remind him of Ann. A gesture, a smile, a scent, and he'd be transported into the past. He'd felt it back then, that he and Ann would be together forever.

And then came the rumors, the half-truths, the betrayal. Covering his wounds as best he could, he'd pretended indifference and broken off with her.

Always in the back of his mind though was the what if. *What if* he found her again? *What if* she hadn't married? *What if* she was available, and this time they made it work?

"Right, Uncle Jack?"

"Um, sorry, dude. What's that?"

Josh sighed. "Didn't you hear any of what I said? You're not a very good listener."

He tried not to smile. The kid was a miniature version of Jack's older brother Dan. Jesus, but Josh acted just like his dad. Bossy and ready to set the world on fire.

"Right. I'll try to do better." He paused, hoping to sound casual when he pumped the kid for information. Nope. He had no shame. None at all. "So what do you think about Ms. Weaver? Is she nice?"

"Yeah. She smells good too."

Jack could attest to that. She'd weighed next to nothing when he'd lifted her for that hug, and she smelled incredible. Like flowers. Lilacs maybe. Lavender? Something purple, if memory served. He could almost see her smiling as she teased him about her flower garden, back when they'd been young and in love.

"Isn't she *Mrs.* Weaver though? Like, she's married or has a boyfriend?"

Josh grinned, a sly smile that warned Jack to be wary. "Dad said you'd ask about Ms. Weaver. I get five bucks."

Jack groaned as he pulled into his brother's driveway. "Don't tell your dad. It was just a question." The boy chortled. Fortunately kids were easily bribed. "I'll give you ten dollars to keep quiet."

"And ice cream after dinner?"

Jack nodded. "Any flavor you want."

Josh seemed to think it over, then agreed. They hooked fingers and, sworn into a pinkie promise, Jack backed out of the driveway and took the little swindler to the grocery store to pick his winnings...where he bumped into another familiar face clearly wishing he'd drop dead. Then again, what else could he expect from the Terrible Trio?

"Well, well. Look who's back." Maya Werner sneered at him. Then she noticed Josh and was all smiles.

Sexy, mean and not his type. He could still appreciate a nice body though. And boy, Maya, like Ann, had only gotten better with age. He wondered if Riley would look as good and figured she had to, because it would never be his luck that women who hated him should turn ugly. Only smokin' hot chicks with friends in town to welcome him back with a boot to the face. Or the balls.

Before he could say anything to Maya, she tousled Josh's hair, glared at Jack, then sauntered over to the bread aisle.

"Who was *that*?" Josh asked. "She's tall."

Just an inch or two shy of him. "She's a good friend of Ms. Weaver's. Or at least, she was back when I knew them." Jack guided Josh toward the ice cream and waited while the boy made his selection.

"Wow. You must be really old, Uncle Jack. You know everybody."

Only everybody who wants to skin me alive. Like it's my fault Ann cheated on me.

Yet some part of him still wondered. Had he pushed her into Chapman's arms? Hadn't they been arguing a lot more as their senior year progressed and the future's uncertainties plagued them?

"Uncle Jack? I'm good."

Jack noticed two gallons of nasty looking flavors in the boy's hands. Bubble gum and cotton candy? "No vanilla?"

"I'm not a vanilla guy." Josh shook his head.

Little did he know, neither was Uncle Jack. Jack's thoughts launched into how amazing sex would be with Ann today. Twelve years of experience and a hell of a lot more knowledge about how to get a woman off. He just knew he could snag her if he could get her in bed.

And then what? Keep her?

The warmth that unfurled from the thought worried him, and he hurried to the register to pay, then drove Josh home.

The next day after waking to his mother's six-thirty wakeup call—did the woman never sleep?—he promised her he'd meet her and his father for breakfast after seeing Josh off to school. Josh, clearly a morning person, had to be uber chirpy about everything, while on the TV an aggravating yellow sponge squeaked and giggled throughout the boy's breakfast. After finally shoving the kid out the door, they made it to school in record time. He walked Josh in, pulse racing at the thought of seeing Ann again.

Ann ignored him, even though he lingered to be noticed.

Playing hard to get. Fine. I'm down with that. He smiled and said in an overly loud voice, "You look *super* pretty today, Ms. Weaver. Have a nice day." He heard her class giggling as he left.

Sexy redhead annoyed. Check. She might be pissed, but at least she was aware of him. Time to meet his parents.

At a popular diner downtown, he sat at their table and stared through the window at the passersby, amused to see so many people wearing high-end clothing. Ah, life in Bend. Did anyone spend less than three hundred dollars on a coat around here? Talk about trendy. Then a few hipsters in dreads and *shorts* and carrying skateboards passed. He loved the contrasts of this town. Rich, poor, liberal, conservative. A whole cross section of America standing on the street corner waiting for the light to change.

"Your brother and Julie are having a baby."

He snapped back to see his mother, Laura, smiling at him. "Really?" He laughed. "I'm going to be an uncle again?"

His dad nodded. "Sure are. That's what happens when it gets cold in Bend. The population booms."

"Oh, Sam, hush," his mother admonished while blushing. Then her eyes narrowed on Jack. "So when can we expect some from you?"

He groaned. "Ma. Not again."

"You're thirty years old, mister. You're not getting any younger."

He looked to his father for help, but his old man grinned. "She's right. You're practically ancient. And so ugly. I mean, really. I might have a few desperate friends' daughters I could set you up with, you poor, lonely soul."

Jack shuddered. "If you love me, keep those crones away."

Laura glared. "I know you're both referring to Kim and Juliette. I don't appreciate the humor."

The waiter stopped by with a pot of coffee, and Jack thanked him profusely. "Great timing. I was needing this like you wouldn't believe."

"No problem, man."

His mother didn't wait for the guy to leave. She continued to lambaste Jack about her great friends, their beautiful daughters and how he'd be doing the world a favor by giving the world future Blooms.

The waiter didn't even bother trying to hide his grin.

"You think this is funny?" Jack asked, knowing it had passed funny and entered pathetic a lecture ago.

"Heck yeah. I got the same spiel from my mother last week. But hey, my girlfriend and I are taking it slow."

"At least you have a girlfriend," Laura huffed. Then she eased back on the annoyance. "Say, you don't have any single woman friends, do you?"

Jack choked on his disbelief. His mother had no problem embarrassing him, herself, her family, hell, the *world*, it seemed, if it would get her more grandchildren.

"Sorry, ma'am. Nope." The waiter smirked at Jack. "What can I get you?"

"Besides a muzzle for my mother?" Jack muttered, "I'll have the number three."

His parents ordered, and after the waiter left, Jack watched his father subtly wipe tears of mirth from his eyes.

Jack sighed. "I thought this was a welcome home breakfast. Not an intervention for your 'pathetic loser son'— who just happens to have his doctorate in environmental engineering, thank you very much. Mom, what gives?"

"I'm just teasing." It hadn't seemed like teasing. "How is your social life, anyway?"

"Um, okay, I guess. Like I told you, I broke up with Beth before leaving Seattle. But we were on the outs anyway."

Laura tsked before taking a sip of her coffee. "That's too

bad."

"Please. I know you couldn't stand her. Another reason I broke it off, if you must know."

His mother raised her gaze to his and blinked. "Oh?"

Sam laughed. "Get off it, Laura. The boy has a mind of his own. We'll be getting those grandkids from him in his own time. That's if watching after Josh doesn't scare him off."

"I love that kid." Jack smiled. "He's a little too much of a morning person for me, but I'm adjusting."

"He's so pleased to be in Ann Weaver's class." His mother beamed. "You know, *she's* still single. Such a nice girl. Whatever happened with you two, anyway? You were in love one minute, then dating someone else the next. I always liked her."

He shifted in his seat. "The typical high school drama. Too young to settle with just one girl. It was our senior year, and we were going in different directions after graduation. Same old, same old."

"Now you're back. And you're single. And she's single…"

A glance at her had him rethinking his strategy to win Ann over. Why not use his mother's knowledge? A smart guy knew when to bend. Besides, it might get her off his back about finding someone else. He just had to figure out what he planned to do with Ann once he got her before his mother made plans of her own. "So about Ann… What else do you know about her?"

His father groaned. "You're in it now, boy. Even I can't save you."

"Sam, shut it." Laura leaned closer. "Ann Weaver lives just two streets down from Dan and Julie."

That he knew. And then she filled him in on what he didn't know. Now he just had to figure out how to use it to his advantage.

Chapter Three

Wednesday afternoon Ann sat at her desk, still laughing about the day's events.

Bonnie, a fellow teacher from the neighboring room, popped her head in. "Still here?"

"Almost done." She couldn't help it. She had to tell someone. "Did you hear what Garrett did at recess?"

Bonnie's wide grin turned into a full-on belly laugh. "You mean when he dropped his pants?"

"And introduced everyone to his little butt, the Grand Canyon, and his front, the Eiffel Tower? How do they come up with this stuff?" Ann started laughing all over again, so hard she cried.

Which was how Jack found her moments later, trying to catch her breath.

"Is this good laughter, or hysterical find-me-a-straightjacket laughter? You deal with a lot of kids, so I'm not sure."

Bonnie coughed and wiped her eyes. "Oh, the good kind. Sorry. Can I help you?"

"I'm here for her." His self-satisfied smile turned on—*annoyed*—Ann to no end.

"I teach his nephew," Ann clarified lest Bonnie tell half the school she had a boyfriend. Ann had her eye on the new fourth grade math teacher down the hall. And Bonnie liked to talk.

"Uh huh. Well, I'm off. See you tomorrow." Bonnie winked at Ann before leaving.

Ann groaned. "Why did you have to say it like that?" She glared at Jack. "Now everyone's going to think I'm dating one of my kids' parents."

"Uncle. You're in the clear."

She fumed. "Is there something you want?" His slow onceover made her blush. Damn him. She looked around. Seeing no one nearby, she decided the time had come to tell him off, to get the closure she'd needed for twelve long friggin' years. She stood up and rounded her desk to face him. "I think it's time we had this out."

"I agree." His suddenly serious expression took her aback. No more innuendo or jokey attitude.

"Yes. You had no right—"

"But not here." With that said, he grabbed her by the arm and glanced around.

"What are you doing?"

He pulled her into the small office that connected her class and Bonnie's. He checked the doorknob of Bonnie's room. Finding it locked, he moved back to her.

"Jack? Let go of me."

He released her. "Just ensuring us some privacy." He leaned by her to close the door they'd just come through.

The office wasn't that big to begin with, but with both doors closed, she felt as if they stood on top of each other. The lack of windows and dim lighting didn't help diminish the feeling of intimacy between them either.

She planted her hands on her hips, focused on being irritated instead of nervous at being so close to him. "I got your note that Josh went home with Brian today."

"Good." He took a step closer.

"So you didn't need to come by." She backed up and hated herself for it. When he took another step toward her, she forced herself to remain firm. "I think you should go."

"I thought we needed to talk." He had the temerity to raise his hand and stroke her hair, the same way he used to back in high school, when they'd been young and in love.

"Get off me." Her voice shook, so she cleared her throat and tried again. "You were terrible to me in high school, and I—"

"Let's agree to leave the past in its place. What's done is done. If I can forgive and forget, why can't you?"

She sputtered. "Forgive and forget? Are you—" Before she could add "kidding me," he kissed her. No soft press of the lips, but a hungry, hot devouring of senses as his mouth stole over hers.

Shocked at the wealth of feeling from a simple kiss, she couldn't stop trembling. Her knees threatened to buckle, so she gripped his open jacket to keep her balance. He pulled her in closer, forcing contact between his chest and hers. The man radiated heat, as well as a carnal attraction she was helpless to refuse.

He groaned and put his arms around her. His hands spanned her waist, and when he pulled her closer to his impressive erection, she realized the passion between them hadn't dimmed one iota.

His tongue penetrated, stroking and seeking as he if had a right. Too bad her body hadn't gotten the memo that he was *persona non grata*. Her breasts tingled. Her panties had grown wet. And her mouth refused to close while she welcomed his invasion.

Jack ended the kiss and traced a path to her ear. His hand crept down to her ass and squeezed. "God you taste good." He kissed her neck, finding the sweet spot that only he had ever mastered.

"Jack…" Where the hell was her self-esteem? Her discipline? Her inner mean girl? Lying down spread-eagle on an imaginary mattress, that's where. Calling on every ounce of feminine outrage she could muster, she put a hand on his chest and tried to move back.

Pitiful. Her hand had turned traitor too. Instead of pushing him away, she clutched his shirt and tugged him closer. He seemed far more muscular than he'd been back in high school. So incredibly overwhelming.

"Kiss me, angel."

She froze. She hadn't been called "angel" in twelve long years. Part of her mourned being pulled back to reality, because she really wanted another toe-curling kiss. But that pet name had been too much. She splayed her fingers on his chest and shoved.

He let go of her ass and moved a token distance. Not far, but far enough to allow her to think again.

"Nope. Not gonna happen." Which would have sounded much more convincing if she didn't sound as if she'd just left a wind tunnel.

He stared at her mouth. "You sure about that?"

"Like you said, the past is the past."

He frowned. "Ann… We were kids. Kids make mistakes. Why can't we start fresh?"

How was he not getting the message? And why the hell couldn't he do the right thing and just apologize? Was "I'm sorry" too hard to handle?

At that moment it became imperative that he feel what she had. The loss, the confusion, the panic when she'd realized she'd been pregnant and lost it before she could come to terms with having been pregnant at all.

"So you want to start fresh?" she asked.

"Yeah. You and me. Let's try it again, the right way."

You planning to dump me in public again? This time I'll be the one calling the shots, buddy. "Okay. But no more kissing in school."

His large grin both charmed and irked her. He was like a duck. Everything rolled off his back. "How about kissing in cars? Or bedrooms? That allowed?"

"I don't get paid by the hour, Bloom. If you want a quick fuck, there are people and places for that. I'm not one of them."

He stared, as if intrigued. "You never used to talk like that."

"Like what?" She frowned.

"It's just… You're so beautiful. Like a fairy queen. But then you dropped that f-bomb. Who are you, Ann Weaver?"

The woman who plans to finally put Jackson Bloom in his place, that's who. "I'm all grown up now, Jack. Accept it."

"Oh, I do." He tapped his heart and looked her over. "I love this new you, all right."

She felt her cheeks heat. Turning from those bright blue eyes, she escaped into her room, never so glad to be in school as she was now.

"So if we're going to do this right, how about a date?" he proposed, hands in his pockets.

She refused to see if his erection had gone down. Looking there would only bring more dirty thoughts that had no place around the story time mat.

"A real date? Not some excuse to justify a night in the great Jack Bloom's bed?" she asked, waiting.

He tried to look wounded. She wasn't buying it.

With a chuckle, he agreed. "You're a real hard-ass, Ms. Weaver. A true redhead with that temper." He studied her from the top her head to her toes and back up again. "How about I take you to dinner tomorrow night? My treat. Josh can stay with my parents."

"Okay." She liked a number of the restaurants in town. And being out and about with him would temper her desire to mount the man like a horse and ride. Talk about having a hard time—*bad choice of words*—not imagining herself on top of him in bed.

"I'll pick you up at six. That work?"

"Sure."

He approached her, invading her personal space once again, and she scowled.

"You are too cute."

Annoyed, she opened her mouth to protest when the devil kissed her. *Again*. Leaving her breathless and aroused.

"Okay, angel. Tomorrow at six. Wear something sexy. Panties optional." He darted out the door before she could smack him.

"Panties optional," she muttered, trying hard not to smile and failing. "What an ass." Thoughts of his fine body had her sighing. "Oh boy, what an ass."

• • •

Ann knew she'd gotten in over her head, so she called an emergency meeting with Maya and Riley at her place. Armed with popcorn and lemonade, she told her pathetic story to her girlfriends and waited for their opinions.

Maya didn't disappoint. "I saw him on Monday at the store. And, girlfriend, he might be a dick, but I get the attraction. That man is four alarm hot. Danger, danger, Ann Weaver."

"Sounds like," said Riley, currently engrossed in her addiction to popcorn. "So he's still a good kisser, huh?"

"Unfortunately, yeah. Even better than high school." Ann stared at her bowl, not hungry. "I mean, if he'd just say he was sorry, that would probably help a lot. But he acts like what happened was no big deal."

"It did happen. Twelve years ago." Riley shrugged. "Hey, don't glare at me. I'm playing devil's advocate."

"More like demon adversary," Maya muttered.

"I'm saying—" Riley glared at Maya before turning back to Ann "—you have to consider that while you had a lot of angst over what happened, he has no idea. Granted, if he'd wanted to break it off with you, he should have done it in private. Involving Selena was cruel."

"That bitch hated us from day one," Maya agreed. "Rich, blonde, always dating the flavor of the week. I'm still not sure what the hell Riley and I did to earn her spite. I mean, you, Ann, I get. You were prettier than she was, not rich—so all the cool kids weren't wanting you for your money—and everyone liked you. Jealousy makes sense. But no one liked me."

"We still don't," Riley said.

Maya flipped her off. "They tolerated Riley, because even back then she baked the best brownies. Not that I see any here. Thanks for bringing some."

"Your ass is welcome. It doesn't need to get any bigger."

"Suck it, Hewitt."

"Please." Riley looked Maya over. "I wouldn't know where to begin."

Maya glared, then broke into laughter. "You're good. Snark is such a fine art, and you're way better than our nice little Ms. Weaver." In falsetto, she mocked, "Oh, Jack, kiss me, please. You broke my heart once, I'm dying for you to do it again."

Ann growled. "Hey. I'm trying to get some help. It's not my fault he's a good kisser."

"You two have chemistry," Riley agreed. "Hard to deny

that."

"True. He's handsome, despite the fact he's an ass. You want your revenge, use it to your advantage, girl." Maya nodded. "Make him pay for what he did. Use him and lose him. Play with him. No one's arguing that he's a ton of eye candy."

Riley sighed. "You got that right. I saw him on the street yesterday. And, girl, he is just…wow. Like melted butter on a peach muffin."

"Great. Now I'm hungry for something sweet." Maya looked around for snacks on the table and spotted nothing but popcorn and peanuts.

"So I should use him for sex then dump him?" Ann felt a moment's guilt. "Doesn't that make me no better than him?"

"Pretty much." Maya took a handful of peanuts, chewed some, then put the rest back. "Ugh. No salt."

Riley shook her head. "Really, Maya."

"Oh please. I washed my hands. Look, Ann, the guy did you wrong. Stop wussing out and take control of your life. Remember our talk a few days ago? You were all about being powerful and taking charge. What happened to that Ann?"

"Looks like Bloom kissed the fight out of her." Riley looked sad.

"Oh stop."

"Brought down by her own vagina. What a sad, sad story." Maya wiped an imaginary tear.

Ann laughed. "My vagina, my enemy. God, you two are killing me. Okay, I'm still in this. I'll bump him and dump him. Can't say the thought of using him isn't a thrill."

Maya gave her a thumbs up. "There you go."

"Just remember the dumping part," Riley warned. "He's a charmer. I remember that all too well. Just like those asshole Black cousins."

Maya frowned. "Nothing charming about that lowdown,

blackmailer Dex. I'll enjoy destroying him."

Riley poked Ann in the shoulder. "See? That's the attitude you should have. Quit playing nice. He's not one of your second graders. Big bad Jack Bloom broke your heart into tiny pieces."

Now Ann was confused. "You just told me he had no idea of the drama I was dealing with way back when."

"Yeah, yeah. I was talking out of my ass."

"She does that," Maya piped in.

"I'm saying the guy will pull out all the stops to get what he wants. And he wants you."

"He did call me 'angel'."

"Oh, low blow, digging up old pet names." Maya glared.

"He's smart. Manipulative." Riley shook her head. "Sorry, I'm in an anti-man mood. Maybe it's not the best time for me to chime in."

"Why? What happened?" Now that she'd mentioned it, Riley did look a bit stressed.

"Anson popped into my shop today to say hi. That dickhead."

"Oh, dueling oven mitts." Maya laughed. Anson Black had a reputation as a successful restaurateur. "Did you hit him with a wooden spoon or what?"

"He bought the place next to mine." A pause. "He's opening up a 'fine dining establishment'," she added in air quotes.

Ann gaped. "Your arch enemy is moving right next to you?" Ann felt for her. "At least mine is only connected to me through Josh. If he lived or worked right next door, I'd lose my mind."

Maya, the witch, laughed harder.

Riley swore. "Sure. Laugh it up. But I'm not the only one dealing with a Black. Dex is back in town and setting up shop too. At least Ann and I aren't afraid to mix it up with *our* enemies."

"Enemies?" Ann wondered at that. Jack was an opponent, sure. But an enemy? A bad guy? He'd done a bad thing, back when he'd been all of seventeen. *Shut it, nice gal. For once in your life, be strong and stand up for yourself.* Her stupid conscience kept trying to ruin her attempts at being bad.

"Yeah, *enemies*," Maya emphasized. "As in, plural. We need to stick together, ladies. The Blacks are back, and Bloom is making a play. Let's teach these guys that we are no one to mess with. Ann, he hurt you. He pays, end of story. Riley, Anson is an ass who's moving in on your turf. Shut him down."

Riley nodded, her lips tight.

"And I have an old score to settle with Dex, that little blackmailing jerk." Maya stiffened. "That boy's ass is mine. Ann, gotta go. I got an idea or two."

"Me too." Riley smiled, a dark grin that gave Ann shivers. "Time to welcome my new neighbor the proper way."

Poor Anson. And poor Dexter. When the Terrible Trio revved up, heads rolled. Determined not to be less than her friends, Ann knew she had to do the wrong thing for all the right reasons. Teaching Jack a lesson would not only help her get the closure she needed, it would help Jack's future relationships. Wouldn't he be a much nicer guy to be around if he understood that hurtful actions had consequences?

Rationalizing her decisions well into the night, she fell asleep and dreamed about Jack and his kiss, and the heartache from over a decade past. She woke feeling groggy.

Better if she'd only broken a bone back then. Because hurt feelings took forever to heal.

Chapter Four

Jack's conversations had never been so odd, or entertaining. While driving his nephew to his parents for the night, he learned all about some kid who'd become a second grade hero.

"He mooned her and everything." Josh crumpled in laughter, going on and on about butts.

Jack didn't remember his fascination with all things ass, but then, according to his parents, he'd been a handful while his older brother had been an absolute prince. His parents liked revisionist history, because Jack totally remembered Dan being a royal pain growing up. Nice to see Josh acting like a normal kid.

"Then Joy got mad and kicked him, so Josie and Matthew had to tackle her."

"Matthew's the boy you don't like, right?"

"No, that's Matthew R. This was Matthew W."

"Right." His head hurt trying to keep the kids in order.

"Then Matthew W. did this." A glance at Josh showed him making an ugly face. "And Josie slapped his back, and we all waited, but Matthew's face didn't stay that way."

"Bummer."

Josh sighed. "Yeah."

They pulled into Jack's parents' driveway. Before he even turned off the engine, Josh jetted to his grandfather on the porch. Jack joined them.

His dad wore a wide grin. "So, big plans tonight, eh?"

Jack tried to play things casual, but he'd been hard pressed to think about anything but that kiss. Ann Weaver had some kind of mystical hold over him. God knew he couldn't tell her, because she seemed to have a few hard feelings about the way things ended back in high school. On that he couldn't exactly blame her—though in all fairness she'd started it.

Yeah, that doesn't sound immature or anything. He glanced at Josh, blaming his regression on his nephew. "Hey, Dad, make sure Josh tells you the Garrett story."

Josh turned around, bent over and grabbed his ass. "Meet the Grand Canyon, Grandpa."

His father guffawed. Okay, it was pretty funny.

His mother didn't think so. "Joshua Bloom, what are you *doing*?" she asked as she came out the front door.

Josh straightened up pretty fast. "Oh, um, hi, Grandma."

The woman had the nerve to glare at Jack.

"What did I do? The kid got that from somebody named Garrett."

"Hill?" She said the name as if it were synonymous with trouble.

Josh nodded. "Yep. Garrett Hill." He darted inside and yelled, "Can I have a cookie, Grandma?"

"Boy has a nose like a hound dog." His father snorted. "Just like his daddy and uncle."

Jack caught the scent of something sweet when the wind blew. "They do smell good. Thanks for watching him. Wish me luck with Ann."

His mother smiled. "Be nice to the girl. Remember, she's a teacher in good standing in the community. Don't get too pushy on the first date."

"Sure thing, Ma. I'll ask her before I try to hold her hand. And if I take her to a dance, I'll keep a good foot between us. Say, we can even sit together in church. That'll be swell."

His father chuckled, then covered with a cough when Laura glared at him. She turned to Jack and smacked his arm. "Don't be a smartass."

"Yeah, smartass," Josh repeated from just inside the house, holding a cookie.

"Joshua Daniel Bloom, I'll—"

The boy darted inside, laughing.

"Nice mouth, Ma. Dad, witness. When Dan comes home, make sure he knows Josh's potty mouth came from Grandma, not me." He raced away before his mother could yell at *him*. Instead he overheard her scolding his father to stop laughing.

The short drive back to Dan's place and the subsequent walk to Ann's gave him time to think. What the hell did he want with her? Inside her pants, obviously. That was number one. But then what?

He knew better than anyone that one couldn't relive the past. The teenagers they'd once been in high school had long since matured. Well, mostly. He chuckled to himself remembering Josh and his Grand Canyon, then sobered up, trying to puzzle out his feelings for Ann.

He was a man with a man's needs. Though he'd had his share of sex and relationships, being around his family had started him thinking about more than casual hookups or girlfriends who went nowhere. He wanted more than just companionship. He wanted…

Love—a dreaded emotion that constantly plagued him. Ann had been his first love. Not his last, but certainly his deepest. His other girlfriends through the years had never measured up to who he thought should be by his side. A gentle, easy-going redhead who thought he hung the stars and the moon.

He still didn't understand why she'd cheated on him with Terry Chapman. Terry had hated him then and probably still did. A rival in sports and with the ladies, he'd always sniffed around Ann, but she'd nicely shut him down. Or so Jack had thought.

Annoyed and hurt all over again, he shoved the door closed on those memories. What was the point of digging them back out? Yeah, his other girlfriends complained he didn't emote or communicate like he should, but Jesus, did he have to verbalize everything? Some things a guy just knew. Like when to bail on a woman. And some things he didn't want to know. Like maybe he hadn't been as good in bed as he should have been. Or that he hadn't made her feel like he should have.

He'd lost his virginity to the one girl he'd never forgotten. Was it any wonder he wanted a piece of her now? Then, before he'd barely known what to do with his equipment, she'd rocked his world. And with that kiss in her tiny office no better than a closet, she'd done it again.

He wiped his sweaty palms on his jean-clad thighs. *Nerves of steel, Jack. Don't let her see she's got leverage over you.* His old problem with Ann would no longer be an issue. He knew how to please a woman, and from that kiss at school, she responded to him with the same intensity she had always had.

If only he could keep things physical. But already he was feeling hearts and flowers. He wanted to spend time with her. To walk her home after school and talk about her day, make her dinner, rub her feet, watch movies and television while cuddling on the sofa.

Man, his buddies would crucify him if they knew how much he liked the things women seemed to go for. To Jack, a solid relationship involved more than just fucking. Which explained why he was the one always breaking off his relationships while his girlfriends begged him to take them back. He might not always communicate the deep stuff that well, but he was hell on wheels in bed and did romance just right.

Like his last relationship. He'd wined and dined Beth, brought her flowers, went for midnight strolls under the moonlight. She'd loved it, loved him. But there had been no lasting spark. Once the sexual newness wore off, Beth had become a clingy woman needing constant attention. They had nothing else in common other than lukewarm sex.

Hell, she still called to see how he was doing—and they'd been finished for two months. Thinking about it, he put his cell on mute as he walked up Ann's steps.

Nothing about Ann had ever been lukewarm. Hot as hell, passionate, angry or loving. But never boring. What would she be like now? Did she still love horror movies? Did she still have a sweet tooth? Did she still read a book's ending before starting it?

He remembered everything about her. Especially the scent and feel of her. And since that kiss…

With a groan, he tried to get a handle on his stupid emotions and growing erection. *Think about Josh. Think about Mom and Dad. There we go. Nothing stiff on me now.*

He knocked and waited. She answered quickly, looking amazing in a pair of jeans, boots, and a fuzzy blue sweater that brought out the beauty in her eyes. Like his, they were blue, but much darker. They reminded him of sapphires, he'd once told her, and he still remembered her sweet blush.

"Hey, angel. Lookin' good." He smiled and drew her hand to his mouth.

Her lips parted, her cheeks flushed and her breathing grew more rapid. All the right signs. He turned her hand over and kissed the middle of her palm, gratified when she gave a soft sigh.

He winked at her. "Let's go."

"Where to?" She pulled on a vest and zipped up, then let him hold her hand as they left the house.

He thanked his lucky stars for getting an agreeable Ann tonight and enjoyed the brisk air outside as they headed back to his place. "We're going to my house. I mean, Dan and Julie's." He waited to see what she made of that, had all his arguments ready to go.

"Okay."

He blinked. "Okay?"

"Sure. I assume we're going to eat there, right?"

"Ah, yeah. I have some nice steaks laid out. Salad, some veggies. You're not off meat or anything are you?" He looked her over. She was so small.

With a laugh, she shook her head. "Nope. I eat healthy most of the time, but I'm a sucker for Riley's cookies."

"I heard she opened a bakery a few years back. She always did make the best brownies."

"I know." She continued holding his hand through their short walk, and even into the house.

It tempted him, the thought of coming home to Ann—*no, not Ann, some faceless woman*—and their house. Of seeing his wife with child, a little boy like Josh. More and more he'd been having thoughts of settling down, but it hadn't hit him until he'd seen Ann again how much he wanted to make that a reality.

Oh boy. Not great thoughts to be having about an ex-girlfriend who pulled his trigger faster than he could say boo.

"Can I take your coat?"

She nodded, and he slid her down vest off her shoulders, encouraged when she smiled at him. After hanging up their coats, he couldn't hold back any longer.

He stepped right up to her, cupped her face and kissed her.

She seemed to melt into him, and like that, he was hard and ready for her. Dinner could wait. Talk could come later. He needed her *now.*

Except hadn't that been his problem all those years ago? Not seeing to his girl the way she needed to be taken care of? Hell, he'd been seventeen and she'd gotten him so hot so fast. But he'd come a long way. *Not that you could prove it by devouring her two seconds in the door.* He reluctantly pulled back and caressed her cheek.

He deepened his voice to embellish his seduction. "Welcome to my parlor."

She grinned. "Well done."

"Yeah, well, we kiss any longer and I will be well done." To his satisfaction, she blushed when she noted the bulge behind his jeans. "That's all for you, Ann."

"Geez, Jack. You're such a classy guy." She moved deeper into the house. "Nice place Dan and Julie have."

A two-story Craftsman with twenty-four hundred square feet. Julie had decorated the place in an eclectic style chosen for comfort more than style, or so she'd said. It worked for Jack on every level. Then again, he'd be happy sitting on a piece of cardboard if he had a TV the size of Dan's. Time to stop dragging his feet and get his own place. He couldn't live with his brother forever.

"I visited years back, when they were engaged. Didn't see you then." He'd wondered if he might, even then.

"When was that?"

"Hmm, back in the winter, when Bend had that big storm seven years ago."

"Oh right. That was the Christmas break I went with Maya and Riley to Cancun. We had a blast."

"I'll bet." He could just imagine the three sexy young

women in Mexico strutting around in bikinis. A treat for any guy with a pulse. "So, what do your friends think of you going out with me?" Why he asked that particular question, he had no idea. Anything to keep his mind off the image of Ann in a tiny bathing suit though. His dick felt hard enough to break off. Not a great way to show restraint.

She grimaced. "Maya thinks I'm an idiot. She doesn't like you."

"Yeah, I got that impression the other day in the grocery store."

"Riley's reserving judgment."

"I always liked Riley."

She snorted. "You and every other guy."

"Hey, I'm human. It would be a sin not to look at any of you. The funny, smart redhead, the sexy Amazon with attitude and the hot chick who can cook like a dream." Even back in high school Riley had had a reputation for being a genius in the kitchen. Maya, though gorgeous, radiated hostility to anything resembling authority. And Ann—

"Why are they sexy and hot, and I'm funny and smart?" She looked annoyed. His fairy queen's grimace was just too cute, but he knew she'd get pissed if he mentioned he had a thing for making her angry, just to see her expression.

"Well, if I'd said hot, I'd be insulting your feminist side demanding I acknowledge you as something other than your looks. I'm trying to tell you I was first drawn to you by your intelligence and humor."

"Oh." She sounded disappointed.

He grinned. "And your hot little body. Happy now?"

She mumbled something that sounded like "I will be," though that could have been wishful thinking on his part.

"How about dinner?" Time to start his grand seduction. First food and good company, then he'd bring her to orgasm so many times she'd lose count. She'd be putty in his hands,

so when he figured out what the hell he really wanted from
her, she wouldn't be able to say no.

• • •

Ann watched him, trying to figure out Jack's game. If he'd
only wanted her in bed, he could have continued that kiss.
God, the man had a mouth made for sin.

When he kissed, he used everything—lips, teeth and
tongue. He stroked her as if he made love to her whole body,
and even now she was slick, her body ready for him even if
her heart and head demanded she stick to the plan.

The problem was he charmed her without trying. That
smile in his eyes, the quirk of his full lips. Even the firm jaw,
now looking a bit shadowy, added to his appeal. Jack was a
man's man. As a teenager, he'd loved just being with her and
holding hands, but she'd never mistaken him for a boy she
could bend to her will.

A lot like now. He kept her on her toes, taking charge of
the date. His house? *Please.* As if she didn't know what would
follow dinner. Some wine, dessert. Then he'd suggest they go
upstairs where he'd bang her brains out, which was fine by
her. She'd never had any qualms with his skills in bed.

She squirmed behind him, wanting to feel him inside her
again. It had been a long time since she'd had any satisfaction
from a partner who didn't use batteries. Not that she didn't
love Mr. Vibe, but he could only do so much.

"Can I get you something to drink?" he asked.

She followed him into a spacious kitchen. Stainless steel
appliances, mahogany cabinetry, and simple dark blue accents
made the place shine. A terrific granite island, complete with
a stovetop, prep sink and seating for four drew her attention.
She noted the bottles of wine on the counter and pointed to
the red.

He poured her a glass and took a beer from the fridge for himself. After putting the steaks in the broiler, he took a sip from his bottle. "So rumor has it you're not seeing anyone."

She sipped her wine, liking the smooth finish. Jack, or more likely Dan and Julie, had good taste. "That would be correct."

"Right. I mean, you're here with me. The Ann I know—or knew, I should say—would never step out on a guy."

She thought she heard something off in his voice. "You're right. I would never do that." *Unlike some*, went unsaid. She wondered how long he'd been seeing Selena behind her back before he'd broken it off with her.

"It's a pretty immature thing to do, but it takes a while for some of us to grow up."

A lame-assed attempt at an apology? A touch of guilt hit her. Should she take this opportunity to just ask him why he'd been so mean to her back then? Clear the air and forget about her revenge?

"Good thing we're all grown up then," she said, waiting to see how he'd respond.

He turned his head to grin at her. "Some of us are better grown than others. You sure filled out nice, Ann."

Still no apology. She wanted—*deserved*—an "I'm sorry" at the very least.

Instead of demanding his admission of guilt, she teased, "Back at ya."

"I know." He hadn't grown out of that charming arrogance of his. "You should see me wield a spatula…among other things." After he fiddled with a pot of vegetables on the stove, he asked, "Do you still like the same things? How about cooking? Gardening?"

"I'm pretty much the same. I like to garden in the summertime. Small pots, flowers, maybe a tomato plant. Not too much. But cooking?" She scrunched her nose. "Not my forte."

"Good thing I offered then. We won't starve."

The tiny dig stung, which was stupid because she'd just admitted she hated cooking. But Jack seemed so sure of himself. So confident in the kitchen, with a kiss, just breathing. It was imperative she take back some control in this weird relationship.

"What are you making?"

He nodded at the pot. "Just boiling some beets. I like 'em fresh, not canned. The steak will be another ten minutes, I'm thinking. You like it medium rare, right?" Turning to the fridge, he pulled out the makings for a salad.

"Medium rare, yeah." Did the guy have to have a memory like an elephant? What *couldn't* he do well? "So, why aren't you married with three kids already?"

He almost dropped the head of lettuce he'd been holding. "What?"

"You heard me. Do you have commitment issues?" She liked the thought of a weakness.

"Nope. Just haven't met Miss Right yet."

"You mean Miss Right Now?"

"Funny, but no. And before you ask, no, I don't have a girlfriend on the side."

"I wasn't going to ask that."

"Yeah, right. I can almost feel your brain poking at mine." He paused. "You're still not over high school, are you?"

The accusation made her feel small. Most people would consider it silly to hold onto a twelve-year grudge. Yet he didn't know the whole of it, and damn it, she deserved some payback. She'd cried. A lot. What had he done but screw Selena Thorpe before throwing her over too?

Resolving to go through with her plans, she shrugged and pretended his suspicion didn't matter. "Water under the bridge. I thought maybe *you* were holding onto some feelings though."

He frowned, his eyes a bright blue. "Feelings?"

She was thrilled to see she'd gotten under his skin. "You know, resentment that we split up. Maybe a little annoyed that I didn't throw myself into your arms the minute I saw you last week."

He turned around to wash the lettuce in the sink, giving her his back. "Nope. Not even a little."

Liar. His shoulders were stiff. She smiled to herself. Finally, a chink in his armor she could exploit. And she knew just how to do it.

Ann walked over to him and saw him tense even more. Perfect. He'd been in charge of everything so far, but not anymore. She wrapped her arms around his waist and hugged him. He felt like an unmoving block of granite.

"Ann?"

"Just a welcome back hug, Jack. Don't let me stop you from preparing our dinner. I'm starving."

He ripped the lettuce and rinsed it under cold water, tossing pieces into a colander while she kept her arms around him. She pretended to accidentally shift and grazed a large bulge below his bellybutton.

"Oops. Sorry."

"Yeah, right." His deep growl turned her on even more.

Realizing how much fun it was to pull the tiger's tail, she went for broke. No longer willing to be the one seduced, it was time to turn up the heat and see what Jack was really made of.

She lowered her hands to his waist and moved them under his sweater, grazing his tight belly. Wow, was he warm.

"What are you doing?" He remained unmoving, but his death grip on the lettuce was telling. "Ann?"

"Shh. Keep working. I'm watching how you do this."

"How? Can you see through my back?" His voice went

deeper as she grazed his navel.

"I'm not so great in the kitchen," she admitted and dared to unbutton his jeans.

The lettuce, she saw as she peeked around him, was caught in his bloodless fingers. She smiled to herself and slowly parted his fly.

Jack, the great big player, didn't seem able to breathe. "*Ann?*"

"Shh. Keep working. I'm learning a lot."

"Fuck me," he said in a gravelly voice. "What exactly *are* you learning?"

"Tsk tsk. Language, Mr. Bloom."

His chuckle turned to a groan when she palmed him through his underwear. "Jesus, Ann. You're killing me."

"I'm trying to learn how to properly wash lettuce. You're not helping."

"Y-you're..." he broke off when she pulled down his underwear and his cock sprang free.

She gripped it, needing both hands to do him justice, and he swore even as he backed away from the sink a bit to give her more room.

He was breathless when he asked again, "What are you doing?"

"Isn't it obvious? I'm making salad. Now what should we do next?"

Chapter Five

Jack did his best to hold on to his control while Ann held him in the palms of her hands. He'd never once, not in his wildest dreams, imagined Ann jerking him off while he prepared dinner.

"Now what do you do after you get it all wet?" she murmured against his back as she stroked him up and down. So slow, yet those soft hands of hers pulled him closer to the edge faster than he'd come in years. He felt all of sixteen again, coming too soon, too fast, too much with the girl of his dreams.

"Um, Ann, you might want—"

"Stop talking and show me what you can do with a colander," she said, laughing against his back. "My, you sure have a large...carrot...in your pants."

He wanted to laugh with her, but he had to focus not to come all over the sink. And the food. And her hot little hands.

"See, I'd think I should peel the veggies first. Long, slow strokes so I don't tear anything important. The skin is pretty fragile, right?"

She worked him up and down, so slow, then faster. He heard himself breathing in time to her movements, heard too her soft little pants and knew he wasn't the only one aroused.

Which made it worse.

"Yeah. I'd get my lettuce all wet. Put my great big carrot into the bowl, then add some creamy dressing. Do we have any of that, do you think?"

"Oh yeah. Fuck, yeah."

Her hands moved faster, and he had to help her get him there. He put a hand over hers, showing her how to hold him, to put the pressure just under his cockhead, while he moved her other hand to cup his sac and fondle him.

"Let's get some of that creamy dressing ready, hmm?" Her breasts rubbed against his lower back, and he sensed the familiar tightening in his balls. He'd never look at salad the same way again. "When can I taste it, Jack? I'm hungry..."

Her fingers tightened, and he groaned as he came, spurting all over his belly, her hands, the freaking sink. He couldn't stop jerking as she continued to pull his orgasm from him with both hands.

When he'd had all he could take, he weakly nudged her hands aside. Still unable to believe she'd given him a handjob all on her own, he cleaned himself up and tucked himself back into his jeans.

"So when's dinner going to be ready?" she asked, wiping her hands on a towel.

He could only stare, noting the color on her cheeks, the sparkle in her eyes so dark they looked black. She hadn't been unaffected, but her humor and sly tone suggested she'd liked being in control. Having him—literally—in the palm of her hand.

Jack had to clear his throat before he could answer. "Pretty soon." Christ, he'd come in mere minutes. But who could blame him? Even he couldn't hold himself to impossible standards when a woman like Ann fondled him to climax so unexpectedly. He glanced at the sink. "The lettuce is a wash, though. I mean, it's not happening." He didn't want to think where all his mess had landed. Not to mention he'd crushed a good bit of the lettuce when she'd started touching him.

She laughed. The tease. He was dying to feel between her legs, to touch her wet warmth, but she looked so pleased with herself right now he didn't want to jinx anything. He was definitely getting a taste of her for dessert. But for now, he'd let her think she had control. This little game between them felt important, but how it might matter later he couldn't say.

She didn't seem to mind that he'd gotten off and she hadn't. In fact, he'd say she enjoyed it. "No salad. But steak and beets, right?"

"Yeah. I'll find us something else to go with it."

"No, I'm fine. I don't eat much."

He studied her, liking everything he saw. "You wouldn't. You're tiny."

Her eyes narrowed. "Not so small I can't still kick your ass, Bloom."

"Have I told you how cute you are when you cuss?"

"Dickhead."

"Just beautiful."

"Fuckwad."

He laughed at that one. "Gorgeous. Makes me want to lick you right up." He stared at her breasts, pleased to see her nipples despite the weave of her sweater. Then he glanced at her crotch and licked his lips. "I'm thinking I'm going to want dessert. A couple helpings, at least."

"Sure you'll have room for it?" she taunted. "I mean, you just had a lot of lettuce."

"Now who's the smartass?"

She snickered. "I'm going to get more wine."

"Good. You get nice and loopy so I can properly take

advantage of you after dinner."

"Convinced you have me pegged as easy, don't you?"

"How could I have you pegged, Ann?" He checked on the beets so he wouldn't reach for her again. He'd cooked them down earlier, so he needed nothing more than a little warm up and some seasoning. The steaks looked almost ready as well.

"Just because you came like a rocket doesn't mean I'm ready to get horizontal with you. I just thought if you had some ease from that pole in your pants, it would make it nicer to have dinner together without you obsessing about sex."

He gaped at her, not sure who the hell this frank-talking woman was. The sweet natured girl he'd once known had been replaced by a blunt woman who'd taken him to heaven with a few tugs of her hands. She still looked like his angel, but now she had sinful moves.

"You think one orgasm is going to tide me over?" he asked with a laugh. "Think again. I'm good for a few more, angel. Count on it."

• • •

Count on it? Could he be any sexier? Somehow she'd lost control of the situation, even though she'd been the one calling the shots. Because now she wanted nothing more than to feel that big shaft inside her. To watch him come with her, staring into his eyes.

Oh man. All that feeling crap had come back with the sex. How could she get revenge when she already wanted more from him than an orgasm? No looking at each other during sex, she decided. Maybe they could do it doggie style. Or...

"You're thinking too hard." He chucked her chin, and she realized she'd been staring at his crotch. "And speaking of hard… Well played, Ann Weaver. You've got me hooked on your hot little hands. But a taste of my meat and you'll be all mine."

"God, you did not just say that."

"Pretty bad, eh?" He smacked his lips. "I have a lot of meat. Big, juicy meat. Inches thick—"

"Stop!" She tried not to laugh.

"Porterhouse steaks. All I'm saying is that you'll love dinner. The beets are good too. They're both nice and round…under my long, fat spoon."

"Oh wow. That's even worse." She didn't bother to hide a smile. "You have to admit I was creative with your salad."

"You sure the hell were." He adjusted himself in front of her, and she knew she'd never forget this night. She, Ann Weaver, had jerked Jack Bloom to orgasm in the kitchen, of all places. Who said she wasn't an animal when it came to sex? Well, besides her last two boyfriends? And Riley…and Maya…?

More than pleased with herself, she excused herself to the bathroom to wash up, then sat down at the kitchen table and let Jack serve her.

He kept smiling, carnal need in his gaze. But he only asked her about her job. She told him funny stories about her students, including Josh. Jack got a kick out of their second grade exhibitionist, even though the poor kid had been sent home for his behavior.

"So what about you?" she asked him. "What's up with the job transfer?"

"I've been wanting to come back to Bend for a while, but I had to finish my education. Did a bit of traveling around the world. It's been a blast."

"No steady girlfriends?" she found herself asking, then mentally slapped herself for expressing such obvious interest.

"A few. But nothing lasting or anything. I can't explain

it. I just knew we'd part ways before long. It helped that I moved around a lot. After graduation, I traveled to Europe and Asia, working while learning. I lucked into an incredible international program through school. Then I came back, got my graduate and fast-tracked a doctorate."

"You have your PhD?"

"Yeah. That's what's allowing me more latitude in the job search. That and the expansion here at OSU."

"Right."

"How about you? I knew you wanted to teach, but you also talked about being an artist or maybe going into business."

She shrugged. "The business thing was a phase. I was consumed with money for a while."

"Aren't we all?"

She smiled, startled to realize how natural if felt being with him. No awkwardness after their session by the sink. No leering. He looked her in the eye when he spoke and waited for her answer, listening to her. She liked him all the more for it and remembered he'd always been that way—unselfish, interested in her as a person.

Not a good thing to realize since she still planned to bump and dump. *This is about teaching him a lesson, isn't it?* She shelved a returning case of the guilts. *Remember, he has it coming.*

"Ann? You okay?"

"Yeah. Why?"

He frowned. "You have a funny look on your face."

"You mean, like this?" She stuck out her tongue and made a face several of her students had perfected.

He made a face back at her, then they traded juvenile insults about mothers that had her laughing so hard she almost spit her wine all over him.

"Quit nursing that glass. You've been on the same one since you sat down to dinner. I'm on my third beer already."

He shook his head, smiling at her. "But then, you always were a lightweight." Pushing away from the table, he gathered his plate. "You done?"

She nodded and moved to stand.

"No, I got this. You just sit pretty and let me wait on you."

"Hey, a man wants to serve me. I'm not going to say no."

"Exactly." He cleared the table, then brought her favorite dessert with him and set it in front of her. "New York style cheesecake with cherries. And no, I did not make this myself. I bought it from Riley. The minute I stepped into her place, she glared holes through me, even when I confessed I was there for you. That's probably the only reason she didn't spit in the dessert."

She laughed. "No way. Riley would never mess with one of her masterpieces of confection, as she likes to call them. She might have spit at *you* when you left the store though."

"Hadn't thought of that." He sat next to her instead of across from her. Way too close.

"Um, I'm good. You can go back to your seat."

"Nope. I can't. A good host sees to his guest. Open up." Damn. He had taken a forkful of the sweet stuff and held it to her lips. "Go on. Take a bite."

"Said the witch with the apple," she added, making him laugh. She watched him while she put her lips over the fork. The fork came back sparkling clean, and his gaze went dark. He took a bite for himself, not looking away from her.

"More?" he asked, his voice husky.

"Maybe a little."

"Maybe a lot." He gave her another bite.

When she finished, he didn't take any more for himself. He stood and pulled her to her feet, then backed her against the wall and caged her between his arms.

"Um, Jack?"

"What's that, angel?" Oh boy. Not the smoky voice.

"I wasn't done my dessert."

"Good, neither am I."

What she feared came to pass, because her control of the situation shifted dramatically when he kissed her. With only one and a half glasses of wine in her, she couldn't blame the alcohol. No, it was all Jack seducing her into a pliant ball of need.

She didn't know when she'd put her hands on his shoulders or dragged them through his hair.

His hands found her bra and unfastened it before she could think to protest. Then he was touching her breasts, teasing her hard nipples. He kissed and nipped his way to her throat, where he sucked until she moaned, lost in lust.

"I need my dessert," he growled.

Her sweater and bra disappeared. Jack's mouth closed over her nipple. He sucked, and she nearly came.

"Jack, oh God. Yes."

He continued to tease, then moved to her other breast and gave it the same attention. Fingers, lips, teeth—all hurtled her toward an orgasm she hadn't thought to experience so soon.

"Gotta taste you." He tugged her jeans open, and before she knew it, she wore nothing at all. Not even her socks.

"Jack." Just his name. It didn't matter that she was stark naked in the kitchen. That he still wore his clothes and she teetered on the brink of climax. She wanted him so much…

He nudged her legs wider and kissed his way down her belly, nuzzling the trimmed hair over her mound.

"You are so sexy." He took her clit into his mouth, and she exploded.

She cried out as he continued to lap at her, sucking her to a bliss that continued to course through her. When she'd moved past her orgasm into sated exhaustion, he stood and kissed her.

She tasted herself on his lips, and it tied them even more

intimately. She could feel him against her belly, hard and huge and ready for round two. What she hadn't expected was her sudden return of arousal so soon after that supernova of a climax.

"You—naked. That's *my* dessert. And I'm still hungry." He looked her over while he stroked her with callused hands. Nothing soft about Jack, especially not now. "You feel so good. I have to be inside you."

Remember, you're calling the shots this time. Take control. Don't let him— "Yes."

Anticipation glittered in his eyes. When he picked her up into his arms, as if she weighed nothing, she couldn't help feeling owned, taken by a stronger, dominant male. She'd always been on the small side, but Jack's presence, size and stature made her want to submit.

Before her sensible side could reassert itself, he stopped in the hallway and kissed her. He'd slyly moved a hand between her legs, and when he thrust a finger inside her, she moaned in supplication.

He pulled away from the kiss, panting. "I'm going to fuck you so hard." He hurried into a bedroom, put her in the middle of the bed and stripped.

Memories of another time, another place intruded, and she stopped him with a hand to his chest before he could pounce. "Condom."

He blinked. "Right." Diving into the nightstand drawer, he found a packet, ripped it open and was about to slide it over his thick length when she stopped him.

"My turn." She urged him to his back and knelt beside him. He palmed her breast while she leaned down and blew a soft breath over his cock. Jack wanted her. No doubt.

"Suck it," he growled. "Take me deep, angel."

A planted manipulation, using that pet name? Or a man at the end of his patience? She didn't care, because as she opened her mouth to take him inside, his hand crept up her leg, between her thighs, then cupped her pussy.

He jolted into her mouth, surging deeper, and his fingers began sawing in and out of her, rubbing her clit while he sought a place deep inside her that needed more.

"No, stop," he rasped when she took more of him.

His balls were hard knots, his cock thick and salty in her mouth. She knew he had to be on the verge of coming. Then he yanked her off him and rolled the condom on. He flipped their positions, putting her flat on her back under him.

"Jack, what—*oh*."

He thrust hard, buried himself as far as he could go, and she tightened around him instinctively.

"I need to move, but you feel so fucking *good*." Jack rarely swore. That he did so now only reinforced how lost he must be.

"More, Jack."

He didn't need to be told twice. There was nothing gentle about the way he took her, and he watched her as each thrust connected them closer. He'd become part of her body. Her mind. But not her heart. She tried to hold onto that corner of herself that had to be strong, determined never to need a man the way she'd once needed him.

But he wouldn't let her hide as he took her like a man possessed. The hard thrusts, the grunting, the magic of their bodies climbing higher in the pursuit of the ultimate pleasure...

"Watch me, angel. Watch me come hard in you."

She cried out his name as she came again, a mess of emotion while he slammed inside her one last time and stilled.

The look of ecstasy and agony on his face was forever burned into her mind. Jack was handsome, but lost in rapture, he was absolutely gorgeous. He continued to shudder as if he hadn't come not so long ago in her hands.

"Yes. All of it," he rasped as he pumped a few more times, still watching her through shuttered eyes. *"Ann."* Finally done, breathing hard, he leaned down and kissed her. "This. This is what I've been missing."

Feeling the same scared her out of her mind. She was falling right back into the role of that weak girl who'd been heartbroken in high school. No. She refused to pay the emotional price tag attached to this romp. Hell, he'd only been back a few days. How tied could they be to each other?

I can use him and lose him. I know I can.

Yet as he stared into her eyes, she had a bad feeling she was lying to herself. She'd make some excuse to leave, then call her friends to circle the wagons. Time to regroup, to—

"Whoa. Where do you think you're going?" Jack asked with a lazy smile, belied by the spark of determination in his eyes. She tried to move him, but he remained buried inside her. A part of her. And still semi-hard.

"I was going to clean up."

"Now, angel, why would you want to do that?" He kissed her, so slowly, so thoroughly, she forgot all about making her escape and pulled him closer. "That's it. Stay with me. Right here, with me."

Chapter Six

"You've lost your friggin' mind." As always, Maya didn't pull her punches.

Next to her on her couch, Riley sighed. "Give the girl a break. It's not every day you have marathon sex with someone like Jack Bloom."

"Fair enough. So was he better than he was in high school?"

Ann just smiled at Maya. Such a nice way to spend a Friday evening, reminiscing about amazing sex with her friends.

Maya scowled. "Figures. They all get bigger and better looking. Then God gives them staying power and *bam*. How do you fight that?"

Riley raised a brow. "Oh? Does Dex have staying power?"

"I wouldn't know."

Her lofty tone didn't fool Ann. "What happened with Dex anyway? You saw him?"

Riley answered for Maya with a laugh. "While you've been playing tonsil hockey with Jack, Maya's been sniffing around Dex's new studio."

"That's right. He's a photojournalist." Ann remembered the guy's fascination with anything camera related in high school. "A pretty good one, from what Bonnie told me. She's friends with his mother."

"Thanks for sharing," Maya muttered. "And I am *not* hot and bothered. That would be you, Riley, panting after Anson."

Anson and Dexter had been thick as thieves growing up. Cousins who were more like brothers, even after Dex had changed high schools during his last year. The Blacks had often been seen hanging out with each other. She remembered that Jack had been good friends with Anson especially.

"I wonder if Jack has reconnected with them," said Ann. "Wouldn't that be funny? Us against them."

"Against? You mean, all of us, or just Riley and me? Did you manage to disengage from the guy without losing too many body parts? Or is he hiding under Riley's couch, attached to you in an unmentionable place?" Maya pretended to look under Ann.

Riley grimaced. "You have the worst way with words."

"Don't hate, Maya." Ann sighed in remembrance. "I was due a few orgasms."

"A few, she says." Maya pointed at Riley. "And don't *you* say a thing."

Riley raised her hands. "What? That despite your claim you can snap your fingers and get sex you might as well be a born-again virgin? That if anyone is due, it's you, Ms. I-Hate-Men? Nope. Not sayin' a thing."

"Glad to hear it." Maya shot Riley a dark look. "Ann, aren't you the one who came up with the idea for girl power? To get back at the ones who need to pay?" She ran a hand through her long hair. "I'm all for it. But we—as a group— need to remain strong. I'm glad Jack rang your bell. But don't forget he did that twelve years ago and knocked you up."

Riley scowled. "Nice."

"Truth hurts."

Ann sighed. "I know I need to be careful. The sex was amazing. But it's just sex." So she kept telling herself. "We made a date to go out tomorrow night. In public. And honestly, I needed the breather. I have to be able to deal with him without wanting to jump him."

"Geez, Ann. It's happening all over again. You're falling for him." Maya shook her head.

Ann flushed. "I am not. The sex threw me. I hadn't expected it to be that good, is all. He's learned a few moves since high school."

Riley snickered.

"But I'm keeping my head. I'm enjoying his body. Like we said. Use him and lose him, right?"

"Uh huh." Maya sounded less than convinced. "I'm pulling for you. It's just that you're a nice person, and it's hard to go against type. I'm worried you don't have it in you to kick him to the curb."

Insulted, Ann glared at her friend. "I can't believe you just said that."

"She called you nice," Riley repeated.

"I know exactly what she called me." Ann pointed at Maya. "You really called me weak. Malleable. Unable to know my own mind."

"All that from *nice*?" Riley and Maya exchanged a look.

"It's not easy for me to be mean, okay? It would help if Jack weren't so darned sweet. The good thing is he didn't apologize, and that really still pisses me off. If I remember how horrible he was to me back then, I can do this."

Riley rubbed her shoulder. "Honey, are you sure you want to? Maybe Jack being back is a good thing, and not because you can get closure by one-upping him, but by letting the past go. You're different people now. Why not see where tomorrow takes you by being honest?"

Maya blinked. "Are you high?"

"What?"

"The guy dicked her over, and you're telling her to give him the keys to kingdom all over again? He needs to own up to what he did. To apologize and suck up and fucking grovel for treating her like she didn't matter. Then, and only then, can Ann decide to forgive him. But falling for him and dating like they have no bad blood between them is just wrong."

"You're so black and white all the time," Riley griped. "Life isn't like that. Life is full of gray."

"That was deep." Watching Riley and Maya pick at each other, Ann relaxed, glad to no longer be the center of attention.

"Oh? Well, if you're going to label me, at least call me white, because I'm on the side of the angels here. But it's funny, I don't see you playing kissy face with Anson *Black*."

Ann laughed.

Riley huffed. "Kissy face? What are you, one of Ann's second graders?"

Maya suggested she shove her head somewhere that was more or less anatomically impossible.

"Jesus. Anson and I have always been at each other's throats. From day one, that boy has been on my last nerve. What's your excuse? Dex was a nice guy. So he made you go out with him on one lousy date. So what? You told us you had fun, so—"

"So? So the little jerk blackmailed me! Me! Maya Werner."

"Is it just me or did Maya somehow manage to stick 'The Great' before her name that we didn't hear?" Ann teased.

"Hey. I'm trying to stick up for you."

"Oh? Because it sounds like you're scared of Dex."

Maya frowned. "Okay, that is totally two plus two equaling five. We were talking about *you* and your tendency to see the best in everyone, even when they don't deserve it. Can you honestly tell me what Jack did to you back then doesn't bother you anymore?"

Unable to lie, Ann shook her head.

"*Exactly.* So until you grow a pair and demand an apology or take my advice and make the jerk feel a little of what you felt way back when, you need to zip your lip. Or at least take my side against Ms. Shades-of-Gray over here." Maya nodded to Riley.

Riley scowled. "You can be such a bitch."

"Yeah, and I haven't had anything to drink yet." Maya wiggled her brows, which sent Ann into gales of laughter.

"You have to admit she has a point, Riley. Our Ms. Absolutes here knows I'm too easy to forgive, and you're too fair to go for the jugular. She's keeping us on the path."

"But is it the right path, I'm asking," Riley grumbled. "Oh shut up, Maya. I'm done arguing. Now, I'm going to pour you a glass of tea. A nonalcoholic beverage. Then we're going to watch that ghost hunting show and we're going to enjoy ourselves. I think tonight they're spotlighting haunts of the Northwest."

Ann settled in with her friends and wondered what Jack was up to. And if he couldn't stop thinking about their next date either. *Oh man. I need more Maya time. If I keep thinking like this, I'll blow my chances for closure for sure and end up falling in love with the rat all over again.*

She moved closer to Maya, hoping to absorb Maya's need for battle, and tried to will herself to focus on the ghosts on TV—not the ones from her past.

• • •

Jack sat at a quiet table in the corner of a sports bar downtown, nursing a scotch as he decompressed from his week with a seven-year-old. He loved little Josh like crazy, but the kid had the energy of ten kids hopped up on pixie sticks. Since the boy had accepted a sleepover invitation from a friend, and Jack unfortunately had no plans with Ann, he figured he'd indulge in a drink. Just him, his scotch, and the highlights of last week's NFL games on the screen above him.

"Well, well. Ain't this grand?"

He turned around, recognizing the face if not the voice, and grinned. "Holy shit. Anson Black." He stood and accepted the hug from his old friend. "When did you get back in town? I heard you were in Portland."

"Mind if I join you?"

"Hell, yeah. Sit down."

They sat and Anson ordered two beers.

"Thirsty?"

"Dex is on his way."

"Wow. It's like a class reunion. I just got back last week. I've already seen Mike Hanson, Deb Sanders and the Terrible Trio." He didn't want to go into specifics about Ann, especially since he had no idea what to do about her.

Anson grinned. "Ah, yes. The Terrible Trio." He looked a lot like he had in high school. He'd gotten a little taller, had put on some muscle and wore his dark hair longer, but his green eyes and mischievous smile hadn't changed.

Dex entered and spotted them, giving an identical grin. The Blacks had always seemed more like brothers than cousins. Except now Dex dwarfed them both. He had to be a good six-four, had a military short haircut and gray eyes that missed nothing. "Damn. The gang's all here. It's like I never left."

"No, you left. You for sure weren't this big in high school. Who'd you eat?"

"My drill instructor."

Jack stood to give him a hearty hand-shake, but like Anson, Dex pulled him in for a bear hug. "Can't. Breathe."

Anson laughed. "Let him go, you monster."

They all sat together with dumbass grins on their faces.

"It's been too long." Jack finally felt as if he'd come home again. Being with Ann had been magical, but the woman watched him with as much caution as lust. Dex and Anson treated him like a long lost brother. He'd missed that familiar connection of likeminded friends.

"So you're back too. All three of us in town again. Like old times." Dex winked. "Especially since I hear you and Ann are a thing again."

"No kidding?" Anson nodded. "You work fast. Thought you said you'd only been in town a week."

"Where did you hear that?" Jack asked Dex.

Dex shrugged. "Friend of a friend who has a kid in Ann's class. I heard all about Josh's uncle who's calling Ms. Weaver pretty. So gross. Ew—at least according to my six-year-old snitch."

Jack grinned. "She is pretty."

"I bet. She always was a sweetheart. I never understood why you broke up."

Neither did I.

Jack continued to waffle over the idea of getting everything out in the open with Ann. But part of him didn't want to know that he'd been the reason for their breakup. Granted, he'd been a kid back then, but he was a man now with a healthy sense of pride. Hearing he'd been awful in the sack wasn't high on his list of high school confessions.

Best to let the past lie and start fresh. Besides, from what his mother told him, Ann had matured into a stand-up woman. She had an impeccable reputation at school and the kids all loved her. She'd had several single men ask about her but she was picky about who she dated. God love her, his mother had friends in all the right places. Apparently Tanya Weaver, Ann's mom, worried about her daughter ever finding a spouse. Something Tanya and Laura had in common—a longing for a bazillion grandchildren.

"Yo, Jack."

He blinked at Anson, who frowned at him.

"You okay?"

"Fine. Been a long week." He took a long sip of scotch. "I've been watching my nephew while Dan and Julie are away. That kid has aged me in ways I didn't think possible."

Dex snickered. "Kids. You gotta love 'em. I'm in the photography business, and let me tell you, taking kid portraits requires a lot of patience."

"I thought you were a photojournalist."

"He was," Anson answered for him. "But the boy wants to settle down. My aunt is putting the thumbscrews to him about living closer to home."

"Please." Dex flushed. "Mom loves me, but I wouldn't be back here if I didn't want to be. Dude, people *retire* here. I mean, think about it. A good bit of the town's economy relies on tourism. Bend is *the* place for the outdoors. I've missed skiing like you can't believe."

"There is that." Jack nodded, wondering if his parents still had his old skis and boots in the attic somewhere.

"What about you, Jack?" Anson asked. "Why did you come back?'

"Same reason. That and they're expanding the campus, so I've got a terrific job I start next week. I really need a place of my own though. I don't want to hang around too long when Dan and Julie get back. My brother is such a slob."

They discussed different areas in town, since the cousins were also looking to find property.

"We're going to rent together first," Dex said, "while I'm

doing research to buy."

"Not me." Jack shook his head. "I want a place near my parents and Dan. I like the neighborhood."

"Northwest Crossing isn't a bad spot. Too hemmed in for me, though. The lots are too small." Dex shrugged.

"It's closer to family. Though in this town, anything more than ten minutes away is considered too far."

They laughed, and the conversation shifted back to old times. "So you and Ann were hot and heavy in high school. Then it was you and Selena Thorpe." Anson whistled. "Took a lot of balls to hook up with her. Even at eighteen that girl was a barracuda."

Jack winced. "No kidding. We dated for a few weeks before I bailed. She scared me."

Anson nodded. "She was living in Seattle. I did business with her second husband for a while. Poor bastard."

The guys laughed.

"But she divorced him and moved away. Just my luck, when I settled in Portland, I ran into her living there." Anson shuddered. "Can you believe she made a play for me? Wouldn't take my hints, so I had to flat out tell her no way in hell. I mean, I was good friends with her ex."

"Just so long as she stays in Portland," Jack said. "I don't think I could handle her back here."

"I don't think *Bend* could handle her back here." Anson clinked his bottle against Jack's glass. "Now let's talk about what really matters."

They all paused as the announcers discussed the Seahawks' prospects.

Dex looked worried. "I don't know, guys. Think we have a chance this season?"

"My money's on Green Bay," Anson said.

Jack shook his head. "No way. Denver's gonna take it."

"Are you nuts?" The three of them threw around stats

and figures like they were math professors, and Jack thought how in all the years he'd been living, he'd never felt at home as much as he did right now. Only one thing could have made things better—and he was seeing her tomorrow. Their second date, and hopefully just the beginning of many more to come.

By the time the guys headed out, Jack had promised to meet up with them that Sunday to watch a game together at his brother's place. Julie and Dan were due back tomorrow, but he didn't think Dan would mind. His brother had mentioned the game several times, and Julie was the best sister-in-law a guy could have.

Ann came to mind. *Again.* He parked at the house and went inside. Unable to get to sleep, he laid down on the couch. He'd proposed to go on a day hike with her tomorrow, alone time spent away from a bed, so they could get better re-acquainted.

He fidgeted, trying to get comfortable while ignoring his ever-present erection at thoughts of Ann. Damn, that woman got to him. So sweet, yet that dirty side of her had thrown him. He loved how confident she'd been, how sexual and inviting.

In the old days, he'd had to instigate everything. And like the boy he'd been, he had never lasted very long. *Christ. Aren't I too old to be obsessing over my sexual skills?*

For a long time after Ann, he'd done his best to become a man-whore—sleeping around campus, gaining skill and stamina. Always safe, because he'd never been anything *but* safe after Ann, he nevertheless went out of his way to forget her. But no matter how many women he shared his bed with, they'd never completely taken her from his memories.

After being with her again, it was as if he'd never left. All the old feelings had returned, and along with them, that same shame, vulnerability and lust he couldn't tame. He had to pull himself together. He knew he wanted her for sex. God yes. But after much thought, he decided they should date. Casual fun. Then, if things progressed to the point he thought they might, they could have a chance at a future.

His heart pounded, and he did his best to put her out of his head. He thought about how great it had been to see the Blacks, on how exciting it was to finally have his dream job, to be back at last with his family.

But he dreamed about Ann and the beautiful babies they'd make together. And that damn dream stayed with him throughout the next day and well into their hike, making it difficult to remember they had so much unresolved between them.

Chapter Seven

Ann walked behind Jack, grateful he'd slowed his pace. The trail they'd taken near Devil's Lake was one she'd often ventured out on as a child with her family. She hadn't realized Jack had known about it.

"How did you find this?" she asked him.

"Dan told me. He and Julie took Josh not too long ago. We're on one of the harder trails, though."

"Yeah. The two mile loop is way too easy."

"You know it?"

"I used to come out here with my folks. We'd hike and camp a lot."

"Oh. We didn't camp so much. My family was rabid about skiing. It's been a while since I've been to the mountain, though. Too busy with school. You?"

"Not my thing. I don't mind cross country, but—"

"You don't like heights." He grinned at her over his shoulder. "I remember."

Their one and only time on a Ferris wheel had been a disaster. She'd been afraid she'd puke all over him at the county fair, and he'd fallen over himself apologizing for pushing her to ride. Not a great memory. Yet he'd held onto it.

"You remember a lot." She didn't like the sober expression that smothered his smile.

He turned back to face the trail. "I remember enough."

His pace increased, and for a while she kept up with him. But when she tripped on a rock and nearly twisted her ankle, she'd had enough. "Hey, tough guy, wait up."

She could no longer see him since he'd rounded the curve. In the hour they'd been hiking, she hadn't seen a single soul. Though it had turned out to be a nice, sunny day with temperatures in the high forties, the clouds continued to tease them with hints of rain.

"Hey, Jack." Still nothing. She grew annoyed, and she was glad. This was what she'd needed to keep the right perspective. Not the nice, charming, smiling guy who made her question her judgment. She needed the guy who only thought about himself and his needs. It made wanting to teach him a lesson easier to remember.

She sat on a boulder and rubbed her ankle, glad to know she'd only bruised it. She stood, put pressure on it and felt no pain. After taking a few steps, she rounded the curve in the trail. "Jack?"

He didn't answer, probably too far up ahead to hear her. The jerk. When would he realize she'd left her far behind?

She made more than one comment about his complete lack of manners and intellect as she tried to catch up with him and shrieked when something large grabbed her from behind.

"Easy, angel. It's just me." He laughed and set her down when she struggled.

"You asshole." She poked him in the chest. "You scared me."

He stopped smiling. "Sorry. Maybe if you'd been

mumbling fewer insults my way, you'd have heard me call your name a few times. I found something."

"Manners, I hope."

He grinned but didn't respond, just held out his hand.

She took it, not amused when her body lit up from the contact. Blasted chemistry…

He led her off the trail.

"Jack?"

"There's something I want to show you. Don't worry, Nervous Nelly. I have a compass, a map and a whistle. Not to mention my cell phone has a GPS. Come on, it's not far."

She debated whether to go with him, but when he took her to a cave she'd been in before, she relaxed. "The monster cave. I remember this." The large hill before them had a rocky opening, exposing weathered rock under the mountain of dirt and grass overhead.

"I figured we could take a break in here. It's pretty shallow but can keep us dry if it starts to pour." The cave had enough height that Jack could stand without bumping his head. Like he'd said, it was shallow. Maybe twenty feet deep. Enough to keep the inside dark until one stepped into the cave.

As a child she'd played inside a few times and loved the feeling of isolation while still being a part of the nature around her. So she entered without reservation. She turned and looked out at the trees and shrubs around them. Deeper inside, a few large rocks would serve as seats.

"God, I haven't been back here in forever." She smiled and took out her camera.

"Doubt you'll get a clear picture in the dark." He stood in shadow.

"I will. You'll see." She stood back with him in the darkness and took a shot of the mouth of the cave, full of light. At the right angle, the jagged rocks near the opening's ceiling looked like teeth. The kids would like that. She'd have them write a story about a monstrous cave next week for class.

Jack's warmth surrounded her from behind. She took another shot, but he refused to let her move away.

"Jack?"

He hugged her. "I missed you last night. Did you miss me?"

His husky voice had an unnerving ability to arouse her. Just the hint of his interest and the feel of his strong arms and she wanted to jump him. *So* not the way to play hard to get.

"Maybe." There. That was better, more standoffish.

He chuckled and lifted her hair off her neck, where he kissed her, nipping lightly. "Just maybe?"

She trembled and would have moved out of his arms if he hadn't tightened them around her. "Jack…"

"Why so tense, angel?" He delved under her shirt to caress her ribs, and she grew breathless.

"W-we're outside. Anyone could see us."

"In the dark? I don't think so. It's just you and me out here." He kissed his way to her ear and whispered, "Let me make you feel good, hmm?"

Before she could say yes or no, he cupped her breasts. She swayed in his hold, and he teased her into breathy moans and pleas for more. God, he made her crazed when she should have been pushing him away and keeping an emotional distance.

He took her camera from her and drew her deeper into the shadows with him. When he turned her to face him, he kissed her with enough heat to set the forest around them on fire. Lost to his taste, to his touch, she didn't protest when tossed her jacket, then unfastened her bra and cupped her bare breasts under her shirt. He pinched and teased as he kissed her, his tongue penetrating her with a slow, lazy taking.

"Oh yeah. That's how I'm gonna do it. Get deep inside you," he whispered before invading her mouth again. He didn't ask—he took. And that dominance aroused her like nothing else.

Jack continued to seduce her as he unzipped her jeans and pushed them down along with her panties, exposing her to the cool damp of the cave.

"I can see your ass in that sliver of light. Man, you are one gorgeous woman. I want you like crazy."

She heard his jeans unzip, let him take her hand and wrap it around his cock. He felt huge and hot. "So thick," she said while he continued to kiss her and pump into her hand. "So warm."

"I want you to touch me. Grip me harder. That's it. Stroke me up and down, angel. God." He groaned while she jerked him off, his hands busy at her breasts again. Each tug and pull of her nipples turned her on that much more.

Jack must have sensed it, because he pulled away from her, then backed her up a few steps and turned her around.

"Jack?"

"Put your hands on the wall and bend over." He sounded as if he'd swallowed gravel. "I need you. Right now." She heard something tear. A condom packet. And like that, he was there, prodding her backside, then lower. He pushed inside her wet channel, his thick cock spearing her with ease.

"*God.*"

"Fuck, yeah."

The tight angle made him feel even larger inside her as he took her with a desperation she felt right to her bones. Her slight moans, his raspy breathing, and the slap of flesh were the only sounds to be heard apart from the rustle of leaves beyond them.

She felt so decadent, so naughty having sex out here. Anyone could come upon them. Though she'd never been one for exhibitionism, Jack's desire, his pressing need for her, gave her a power she didn't want to let go.

"You feel so good." He sawed in and out of her, his thrusts growing deeper. Faster.

She clutched the cold, damp wall for support as his taking grew rougher. He let go of her hips with one hand to reach around her, and his nimble fingers found her clit.

In seconds she shattered and cried out, unconcerned anyone might hear.

"Yeah, that's it. Come hard." Jack gripped her waist and hammered into her, taking her to her tiptoes. Then he jerked once more and stilled, his climax apparent in his stiffening frame.

A moment later, he eased out of her, and she pulled up her panties. After some struggling, he refastened her bra and set her shirt and jacket to rights. She turned to see Jack watching her, wearing a wide grin. Standing at the mouth of the cave, he had enough light on him to show his satisfaction.

"Not how I planned to spend my Saturday, but I'm sure as hell not complaining."

Feeling defensive, she planted her hands on her hips. "You're the one who dragged me in here. You were the one with the condom. Sounds like a plan to me."

"Yeah?" He raised a brow, and she wanted to slap his condescending face, then kiss him until they were rolling around on the ground. "You're the one flaunting that tight ass and those breasts."

"Flaunting? Under jeans, a jacket and long sleeved T-shirt?"

"I have a good memory." He studied her. "I can't stop thinking about the other night. Now I can't stop thinking about what we just did. Let's go back to your place and spend some time in bed."

Where he'd make her forget all her reasons for keeping her distance. Just coming down from a sexual high and she wanted to hold hands and cuddle with the man. For all that she wished she could turn off her emotions and fuck, it just wasn't happening.

"You frustrate me, you know that?"

He snorted. "Join the club. I get hard just being near you. And this is only our second date."

She blushed and hoped he couldn't see it. *Oh hell. I'm easy.* Two dates, and she'd had sex with him on the first one *and* on the second.

"Watch your tone or you won't get a third," she snapped, out of sorts and not sure who to blame.

He chuckled, but the laughter sounded forced. "Honey, I could have you flat on your back again right now if I wanted. But I—"

She stepped forward and poked him hard in the belly. "Dream on."

"Hmm. Want to bet?" The gleam in his eyes warned her to tread warily, but the redhead in her said *screw it* and took his dare.

"Yeah. Let's bet. We'll head back to my place and see who has the other one begging for a fuck."

His eyes narrowed. "You know you get me hard when you swear like that, don't you?"

"I do," she said and licked her lips. "Lightweight." She cupped him between his legs and squeezed, keeping her hand there. Wonder of wonders, he started to harden again. "Like I said. Easy."

She would have pulled her hand back, but he kept it there. Then the bastard kissed her, and his punishing kiss had her moaning into his mouth before he pulled away.

"Say what you want, but I know what you like, Ann. A little rough touch gets you wet, hmm?" He gripped the hand holding him. Then as suddenly, he let her go. "So this bet, what's in it for me when I win?"

"Whatever you want." She crossed her arms over her

chest, clenching her hands into fists so she wouldn't touch him again. "But you won't win. What about my prize when I make you come?"

His nostrils flared as he stepped closer. "How about winner gets the other to do whatever he wants for twenty-four hours?"

"You mean whatever *she* wants."

He smiled. "Dream on, angel. I know what I'll have from you. A few blowjobs." He put his backpack back on, though she hadn't seen him take it off.

"A few?" she asked as he handed her the camera.

"Then I'll have you ride me so I can play with your breasts and suck those nipples while we fuck. I know you like that."

She fought to appear blasé. "Oh?"

He laughed. "Yeah, *oh*. Don't even try it. I know when you're aroused. That's the face I want to see." He ran a finger over her cheek. "You're so beautiful. I can't wait to have you right where I want you."

She shoved him back, and as he righted himself, she took a quick picture of him. "That's what I want to see. You off balance and falling at my feet."

He frowned when she laughed. "Let's head back so we can get this bet laid to rest."

They started back, this time with her leading the way.

"I take it I'll collect my winnings next week?"

He snorted. "You mean *I'll* be taking *my* winnings. And yeah, next week. I'm thinking Friday night to Saturday night. I'd suggest we start tonight, but I'm meeting the guys tomorrow, and no way in hell I'm sharing you with them."

"The guys?"

"You remember the Blacks? Anson and Dex? They're back in town."

She wanted to laugh but didn't. It just figured Jack would reconnect with the detestable Black cousins, as Maya liked to call them. Ann thought *detestable* was a little harsh. Personally, she found Anson too conceited for her taste, but she'd always liked Dex.

"A date with the guys, hmm? And here I thought you liked girls." Immature, but she was too tongue-tied to come up with anything better at the moment. Her body was still singing to her.

He yanked on her shoulder to halt her and whispered into her ear, "Girls? No, angel. I like women. In particular, one sexy redhead with a mouth I plan to slip into real soon."

She swallowed audibly, and he laughed. Picking up the pace, she had them back at the car in record time. The drive to her house felt like it happened way too fast, despite the silence between them that even the radio couldn't fill.

Once inside, Jack closed the door behind them and slammed her back against it. Not hard, but with enough force to show he meant business. He gripped her hair and tilted her head back, then kissed her until she couldn't breathe.

He didn't wait or ask but shoved his hand down the front of her pants and slid his fingers between her folds.

"Yeah, so wet. I know just what you like." He grinned against her lips before kissing her again. His fingers worked their magic, never letting up until she exploded into an intense orgasm without warning.

He eased the pressure against her clit but didn't take his fingers away. Pulling back from her mouth to stare into her eyes, he smiled. "And that's just the beginning."

"Ch-cheater," she accused while getting her breath back.

"Angel, haven't you heard? All's fair in love and war."

Chapter Eight

Ann still didn't know how he'd done it. The Wednesday following their bet—a bet that she'd *lost*—she watched her class empty of chatting students and cleaned up the room, all while thinking about Jack.

As if the to-die-for sex wasn't bad enough, he'd sent her roses. *At work.* She'd had to explain to the front office and a few nosy coworkers that a man with a misguided crush liked her. The only good thing to come of her confession had been Trey Atwood's sudden attention. The fourth grade teacher she'd been gathering her courage to ask to a movie had emailed her an invite the next day.

She'd said yes, all the while wondering what Jack might think. "Like I need to ask him for anything. Permission? Please." They weren't dating. Not seriously. Having sex like rabbits? Yeah, that they were doing.

After she'd lost the bet—*had she*—he'd gone home with a smug grin, accompanied by an invitation to "dinner and only dinner" for tonight. For some stupid reason, she'd said yes. A smarter woman would have stuck to strictly having sex. But not Ann. She wanted to spend time with him without sex on the table…on a bed, in a cave or against a freaking door. He'd turned her into an insatiable sex fiend.

She flushed. From celibacy to nymphomania in just a few days. How embarrassing she'd turned out to be so needy.

"You going to scrub that desk to death or what?" Maya asked from the doorway, startling a small scream from her.

"Don't *do* that."

"I'll wear a bell next time," Maya drawled. "So Riley and I haven't talked to you in a while." Three days to be exact. "What's up?"

Ann cleared her throat. "Um, nothing."

"Yeah? Then why are you talking to yourself? Why are your cheeks so red?" Maya frowned. "Why does that look like a hickey on your neck?"

Ann slapped a hand over her neck, mortified. "Seriously?"

"No, but the fact you thought there might be one answers one question. You are vaginally compromised."

Ann gaped at her friend and hurriedly dragged her into the classroom. "Keep your voice down. I teach small children here."

"Who were all housed in a woman's body at one time or another. Vaginas are not strangers to them."

"Would you stop saying 'vagina'?"

"How about va-jay-jay? Better?"

Ann groaned then gave into the madness and laughed. "Why are you here harassing me?"

"We miss you. That and I have a bet going on with Riley that you'll cave to the wonder dick and drop your vendetta. She says you'll cave. I'm hoping you'll do me proud." Maya shrugged. "That or you'll end up having so much sex you start walking bowlegged. Then the school will find out what a ho you really are, fire you, and you'll take up hooking down on Wall Street. Sadly, Riley and I will have to pretend we've never met you, and you'll die lonely and alone with only your johns for company."

Ann blinked. "All that from not talking to me for three days?"

"What can I say? I'm in a creative mood. Just finished four new pieces for an upcoming art show."

Ann chuckled. "You artists and your weird senses of humor. Now help me tidy up here and we'll walk back to my place."

After cleaning the room, they left together, thankfully passing no one she knew who might overhear Maya's R-rated mouth. The woman liked to talk at ten decibels above normal whenever it had to do with an embarrassing topic. Namely, Ann's new sex life.

"He's good," Maya said. "I can tell. You actually are a little bowlegged."

"Would you shut up?"

Maya laughed.

"He's great. Awesome. Huge. Happy now?"

"Not as happy as you apparently."

"Well, something you might be interested in, he met with the Blacks on Sunday. One great big happy family of blackmailers and cheats watching football together."

"Figures the snakes would find each other and coil up into a nest." Maya frowned. "So why haven't you been talking to us? Tell me."

"I've been busy." She glanced around. Seeing no one near, she shared with Maya a few details about her weekend.

Maya whistled. "I am now officially jealous. He might be a snake, but he sure seems to know how to do the mambo mattress dance."

Ann laughed and would have replied when she saw Julie and Josh walking together down the street.

Maya followed her gaze as the pair turned the corner.

"Guess Julie and Dan are back. Jack still staying at their place?"

"How—?"

"Small town. Besides, I have my feelers out about our sly adversaries. The enemy is tricky. *Dicky* too."

"That was just bad." They arrived at her place and walked inside.

Maya sighed. "I know. I blame Riley. Girl has been in a funk since Anson's been back. He had the nerve to flirt with her the other day at the bakery. She's PO'd to the point I'm here bugging you instead of messing with her."

"Ouch. I should call her."

"No. You should tell me what I want to hear. That you're sticking to the plan."

"I am," she said, "It's been hard. Having sex without an emotional connection is tough, but I'm trying to keep it separate. We're having dinner tonight. Just dinner. Then, well, I lost a bet. Friday night I'm his for twenty-four hours."

Maya loafed on her couch. "Man. I need to get some action like that. Let a guy try to boss me around for a day."

"Try being the key word. You have control issues."

"I do. And I fully admit it. Acknowledgement of the problem is the first step, you know."

"You're such a dork. Oh, Maya. What do I do? I'm trying really hard not to like Jack again. But he's being so charming. I mean, he's making my toes curl in bed. Then he leaves, and next thing you know he texts to tell me to have a nice day or share something funny Josh said."

"But he still hasn't mentioned high school, hmm?"

"No. He's made a few remarks about putting the past behind us. But it's just…"

"Just what?"

Ann didn't know how to explain without sounding childish.

"Just that you can't get over the hurt?" Maya answered. "I get you. Dex screwed me over in twelfth grade. And you know what? Over a decade later I *still* want to put a hurt on him. My mom dropped the ball when I was a baby, and now I have commitment issues. I'm twenty-nine, so clearly I'm not over that yet."

"We're not crazy for feeling hurt after so much time, are we?"

"Nope. We're normal. We just need closure—hence the revenge."

"Right. Revenge." But on who, Ann wondered, because trying to remain emotionally detached from Jack seemed to wound *her* more than him. "Well, it's early yet. I've only been with him a week or so. He's barely been back."

"He's been here long enough to have you on *your* back."

"Crude, Maya."

"Yet true. Look, have fun. Enjoy him a little. Enjoy him a lot. Just don't lose yourself to him again. For all you know, he's fooling around with you while secretly engaged to Selena Thorpe."

Ann grimaced. "Must you say her name?"

"Sorry. My point—don't trust the guy. He hasn't earned it."

They talked a while longer, then Maya left to get back to her studio.

After a call to Riley to say hello, Ann left a message then went out to clear her head. She returned in time to get ready for her dinner with Jack and met him downtown.

Jack waited for her outside Noi, the new Thai place she'd been dying to try, talking and laughing with someone. He waved her over.

"Hey, Ann. You remember Dexter Black? Dex, Ann Weaver."

"Oh my gosh. You are *huge*." Ann goggled at Dex, who

used to be almost Ann's height.

"Yeah, yeah. I hit a weird growth spurt and it forgot to stop." Dex kissed her on the cheek. "You look terrific, Ann. Why don't you ditch Jack and come out with me? I'm going to see a movie. A drama. With subtitles," he added hopefully.

"I would, but I think Jack might cry if forced to eat alone."

Jack frowned at Dex. "Hey. She's with me."

Dex rolled his eyes. "Whatever. Anyway, see you later. Bye, Ann." Dex started walking away, then stopped and turned back. "Hey, tell Maya I said hi when you see her." He gave her a mocking salute as he left.

"Yeah, that'll go over like a lead balloon."

Jack heard her as he ushered her inside the restaurant, because he grinned and said, "Let me guess. Still not over Dex blackmailing her into going to his prom, eh?"

"If you know Maya, you know she holds grudges."

"Gee, Ann. She was so nice to me at the store last week. I can't imagine Maya would ever be brutal, in any situation."

"Funny. So let's have dinner."

"Right. With our clothes on." He said that a little too loudly, because more than one person turned to them.

Flushing with embarrassment, she punched him in the arm.

He chuckled. "Sorry. Hey, our table's ready."

They sat down and ordered. After a while Ann realized they were still studying each other. Jack shook his head.

"What?"

"I still want to do you."

"So romantic." She tried not to blush but couldn't help the burst of pleasure that came with being found desirable.

"I'm trying to have a casual dining experience here. But all I can think about is last Saturday…"

When he'd made her scream his name. Talk about a talented tongue.

"So what do I have to look forward to this weekend?"

His wicked grin confirmed her worst fears and dampened her panties. He wouldn't go easy on her. Especially now that he knew how much she liked being bossed around. And spanked. And having her hair pulled.

"Oh, I have a few things in mind." He paused. "Is it just me? Or did it get really hot in here?"

"Stop." She looked around to make sure they weren't being spied on, then focused on him again. His eyes were so blue. Even the stubble on his chin looked sexy. She wondered if he knew that and forced himself not to shave just to grow that stubble.

He watched her without blinking. "What?"

"What what?"

"I like the way you're looking at me. Like you're so in lust you can't see straight. That or you're just really hungry for dinner."

She blew out a breath. "I thought this was a casual date. Talk about something other than sex." Inspiration struck. "Tell me about your parents. Or Dan and Julie. How was San Diego?"

Jack sighed. "Yeah, that'll kill the mood. Dan and Julie are great. Apparently the trip went well." He discussed his brother's job and his sister-in-law's amazing capacity for tolerating Dan's neuroses. "Julie just laughs at him. I'm surprised each and every time I see him alive after he leaves his dirty socks in the living room."

"True love. The ability to look past laundry." She snickered.

"Smartass."

The waiter arrived with their food and they dug in.

Jack pointed his fork at her. "So tell me about your family. Your mom and dad are okay?"

"Great. In Europe through Christmas. They're still in

love after nearly thirty years. That's the exception these days, not the rule."

"Exception?"

"Couples who don't divorce. It's depressing. What's the point of dating, you know?"

He gave her a naughty smile. "Oh, there are merits to dating." At her look of disgust, he laughed. "Come on. It's nice to have someone you can trust that way. Intimately, I mean. But think about it, Ann. Coming home to share your day. Movies, dinners, spending time together with someone who loves you and can show you in so many creative ways."

She glanced down at her plate, uncomfortable with the way he seemed to be looking at her. Had he seen the longing in her eyes? She sure hoped not. Granted, a fantasy of him being her special someone was all nice and good, but far from reality.

"Isn't that something you want?" he asked.

She nodded and continued to concentrate on her plate. "Eventually. I don't know. Relationships are a lot of compromise. My parents argue then spend their time making up with kisses and laughter. They've had their ups and downs. But their relationship is so true, so real. I'm just worried I'll never find something like that." She stopped herself from rambling, mortified she'd been so candid. But when she chanced a look at his face, she saw only his understanding.

"Tell me about it. Not only do I have my parents to deal with, I have Dan and Julie. My folks are celebrating their thirty-fifth anniversary this year. Dan and Julie their tenth. And me? I'm the loser who broke up with yet another girlfriend. My mom is on me about grandkids daily, as if Josh and Julie and Dan's next one isn't enough."

"Julie's pregnant?"

He smiled. "Yep. I'm going to be an uncle twice over."

"That's terrific. Congratulations."

His goofy grin brought down another part of the wall holding her heart safe from him. How could she not feel such affection for a man who not only rocked her world, but doted on his family? She loved children, and clearly Jack did too.

Then she remembered that they'd once almost had a child between them. And it shocked her, because she never dwelled on that time in her past.

"Hey. You okay?" He sounded concerned.

She forced herself to cough to explain the shine in her eyes. "Sorry. Hot pepper."

He relaxed. "Good. I mean, I thought I'd said something to upset you. Not my fault. I told you not to order the hotter stuff."

They teased good-naturedly, argued over the bill, which he insisted on paying, then ended the dinner with a plan to meet again Friday night.

"Remember," he said as he walked her to her car. "I won you. You're mine for twenty-four hours. Friday to Saturday night. Your place, because, yeah, I'm still living with my brother. And no way I can do all the things I want to with my nephew in the next room playing with Legos."

"Good point. But I don't think winning the bet entitles you to my house too."

"Sure it does." He stepped closer, backing her against her car. "Every part of you is mine Friday night. You have no idea how hard it's been waiting." He fused his body to hers, so she felt exactly how *hard* it had been—and still was.

The kiss, when it came, demanded a response, and she gave it to him. Moaning into his mouth, clinging to his shoulders, she felt possessed.

He pulled away slowly and smiled. She just stared, wondering how he continued to do that. Melting her into a puddle of obedience with a kiss.

"Oh yeah," he promised in a low voice. "I'm going to own

that pussy, that mouth and that ass Friday night."

She swallowed hard, trying not to be aroused and failing miserably. "Ass?" she squeaked.

His menacing smile aroused her. "Don't worry. I'll be gentle. At first." He kissed her again and stepped back. "See you soon, angel."

"Again with the angel," she muttered, watching him walk to his car. She got into her own and sat there, tapping the steering wheel.

The man was dangerous, no two ways about it. He played her like a master, and she kept falling for his moves. The sweet pet name. The fiery kisses. The incredible smell of his cologne that lingered just under his skin. Not overpowering, but seductive all the same.

How could she protect herself from the man if she found herself falling for him all over again? And after Maya had bet money on her...

Laughing to herself, a bit hysterically, she did her best to pretend they had nothing between them but sex.

And knew she was telling herself one whopper of a lie.

Chapter Nine

Friday night. Jack knew he'd arrived early. He didn't care. He hadn't been able to think past the idea of having Ann under him for the next twenty-four hours. Even his introduction to his new job yesterday hadn't dissuaded him from planning on how best to use his time with Ann.

Every minute spent with her only pushed home how right they were together. The hike. The sex—*my God*, the sex. Scintillating conversation, compatible senses of humor… The only thing he didn't like was the way Ann held back from him. He could see the wariness in her big blue eyes when she watched him. He didn't like it. He wanted to see her surrender, to see that the love between them had only been buried, not exhausted.

Tonight he planned to push past her comfort zone into some hard-hitting truths. In between making her come and cry out his name.

He grinned to himself and pressed the doorbell.

A frown answered him as the door opened. "You're early."

Ann wore a robe and had her hair up in a bun that made him hunger to take it down—but only after he'd kissed, sucked and licked every inch of her first.

"You're not dressed." He forced a frown. "Did we or did we not have a bet?"

"Oh, stuff it. I'm still getting ready. Go sit in the living room."

He swore he heard her say *jackass* before she stomped down the hall and disappeared.

A glance around showed him more of Ann. The house was cozy. Neat, comfortable and colorful. She had a few pictures of her family and friends. None of him. But then, why would she? Still, it bothered him. He wanted to see a few photos of them smiling together. Them backpacking, touring Germany, France. Taking in a sunset at the beach. An awesome fantasy of a future he'd once dreamed about.

As he'd feared, coming back to Bend had been about more than reconnecting with family. Ann had been a large part in his decision as well. He wanted marriage, a family, and the one woman who should have been by his side and wasn't.

Ann's footsteps echoed on the hardwood floor. He grinned as he noticed the shuttered blinds all around. Ann knew he'd go freaky on her from the start. Smart girl. "Are you wearing what I sent you?"

"How did you know my size?" she asked, her voice coming from right behind him.

Remembering what he'd purchased, he felt his blood race, his cock hardened and he had to swallow past the lump in his throat. Pouncing on her would not send the right message. Though he planned on making love to her all night, he needed to pace himself. He wanted her so hooked on his body that he'd be in her mind and heart before she could push him back out. He'd make sure she never looked at another man again for pleasure. Or love and affection.

Now that he'd finally admitted to himself that he had to have her and no one else, he forced himself to relax. *Roll with it. She's yours. Act the part. Be the man.*

He unbuttoned the top of his shirt and sighed. With his knees spread, and relaxing into her couch, he felt like a sultan awaiting his servant and smiled at the thought. "Come here, girl."

"Girl? Really?"

He stifled laughter. "I could call you slave."

"No, no. Girl is fine. Bad enough I really do feel like a harem girl in this stupid outfit." She moved in front of him and waited.

He took his time studying her, wondering if a man could orgasm from sight alone. She wore red high heels, a miniscule black skirt that cupped her ass, and a bikini top that might as well have been a length of dental floss with two tiny triangles for all that it *didn't* cover her. The top barely hid her nipples but allowed him to see her full breasts and taut belly.

"Very nice. Any underwear?" He'd told her to leave it off.

"No."

"How about 'No, Master'?"

"How about 'Kiss my ass'?" she said sweetly.

"Sure thing. Turn around."

She blinked at him. "Ah, I was just kidding."

"I'm not. You don't do what I tell you to, you'll be punished." He spread his legs wider, trying to give his cock some relief from his constricting jeans.

She eyed him and bit her lower lip. So fucking adorable. He wanted to take her and ride her into the first of many orgasms to come. But she obeyed and turned around.

"Good girl. Don't move," he ordered.

She nodded, her hands by her sides.

He sat up and grabbed her thighs, delighting in the silky feel of her legs. "You shaved."

"Everywhere. As ordered."

Fuck. He drew in a deep breath, prayed for patience, and let it out. Then he ran his hands up her thighs to her ass. The skirt didn't hamper him in the slightest when he pushed it up to hug her waist. The stretchy fabric had become his favorite new choice of material for all her play clothes. Because yeah, this woman turned him on, no question. One thing they wouldn't have a problem with—their sex life.

He nudged her thighs wider, and she accommodated him on those heels that accentuated her slender calves. When he dragged his hands over her ass and down the inside of her thighs, he felt the wet heat of her desire. Needing more, he cupped her pussy.

"Jack," she moaned and clenched her small hands into fists.

"You are fucking sexy," he said. "And so mine." He slid his finger inside her, closing his eyes to concentrate on how she felt.

She faltered on her heels as his finger explored. "Oh."

"Don't move," he growled. He pulled his finger out and turned her around. Staring at her clean-shaven pussy, he palmed her ass and pulled her closer. Unable to wait any longer, he shoved his face close and sucked her into his mouth. Her tight clit and womanly scent went straight to his cock.

He licked her and ground his face against the sultry evidence of her need. "Want you to come," he said between strokes of his tongue. "All over my mouth."

"Yes, Jack. Please." She clutched his head, grinding against his lips.

He speared her with two fingers, shoving hard and deep, and sucked her clit into his mouth, teething the nub.

She cried out as she came, and he lapped her up, wanting

to devour her heart and soul. When she trembled against him, he pulled away and unbuttoned his jeans, then slid them down to his knees. He hadn't worn underwear either.

"Sit on me." He couldn't help the deep timbre of his voice, or the slick shine of his cockhead.

"Condom?" she said between breaths.

"Not tonight. Not with you. I'm clean. So are you. You're protected, right?"

"I…" She paused, and he knew if she told him to wear one, he would. Anything to get inside her. "Yeah."

"I mean it. I'm gonna come inside you. You're okay with that?" he asked—*begged*—as he guided her to straddle him.

"Well, only because I lost a bet." Her slight grin relieved him.

And then he couldn't think because the heat of her pussy was over him. He thrust up even as she sank down, and the deep push inside her was like coming home.

"Not gonna last long. Oh fuck," he swore as she rode him. He gripped her ass as he pushed her up and down, her slender body milking him of pleasure. "You feel so good. So good, angel." He couldn't think as she took him past control, until he was fucking her harder, giving no quarter.

He wanted to kiss her again, to suck on her nipples, eat her pussy, all of it. But he couldn't stop the rising lust rushing over him.

She bucked, gloving him in her tight pussy.

He had to be leaving bruises as he clenched her ass, but damn if he could stop himself. He was so close, so—

She slammed onto him one final time and swiveled her hips, and he lost it. "*Fuck.*"

Emptying inside her until he couldn't breathe, Jack forgot everything but Ann. When he blinked his eyes open, unaware of having closed them, he saw her watching him with an unguarded expression of affection and hope. And just as suddenly, when she realized he saw her, the shutter came down.

Annoyed, spent, and needing some recovery time, he arched up into her, loving the feel of surrounding heat. Still half-hard, he refused to pull away.

"You feel good?"

She nodded, looking shy.

"Tell me how much you like my cock. Use the words."

She colored but repeated his words.

"Tell me what you want me to do next. You want me to fuck that tight ass? Come down your throat?" He dragged his hands over her back and up, then circled to her front. He pulled down the left triangle hiding her nipple and sucked until it stood ramrod stiff.

She rocked over him, and the sudden return of a full erection didn't surprise him. He could go twice, quick back-to-backs, if he could stay hard long enough. Obviously not a problem with Ann.

He let go of one breast, covered it up, and exposed the other. That one he pinched and tweaked with both fingers and teeth until she was a writhing, moaning mess.

"You like what I make you feel?"

She nodded, but again he wanted the words.

He gripped her hair and pulled her head back, aware of the choppy breathing and tightening of her body around him. Ann liked it rough. Kinky. And that made him like her even more.

"Tell me exactly what you want, angel. Or you're going to feel this cock up your ass without the lube you're gonna need. Maybe you want it to hurt?"

She clenched tightly around him, and he swore to himself he'd make this second round last.

"I love when you grab my hair and tug. Or when you bite and slap my ass," she confessed. She rocked over him, her motion jerky. "I want to feel you come inside me. So hard," she moaned. "Fuck me."

He took her nipple in his mouth and bit down, not to hurt, but enough to be firm. Sucking her wasn't easy with her moving faster over him, but he held on and slapped her ass.

"Yeah. Oh yeah, baby." She gripped his head and ground over him.

He couldn't breathe, lost in lust and love. Ann might look sweet and innocent, but beneath the good girl clothes was a kinky woman who loved pleasure and took what she wanted.

He let her nipple go and shoved his face into her neck as he dragged her down over him and shot inside her again. So much need for this woman he couldn't contain.

She kept rubbing herself against him, dragging out his orgasm, until she moaned and came with him.

The marathon sex should have tired him out. Twice in maybe half an hour. He almost wished he might have been done, because the woman would wear him out if he weren't careful.

When he pulled his head back to look at her, he saw her satisfied smile. He wasn't prepared for her tender kiss, or the way it deepened.

"That was amazing," she said on a sigh. "You made such a mess inside me, but I don't care. I don't think I'll ever move again."

He laughed with her. "Jesus. Me neither. You feel so good around me. You just don't know." He leaned his head against her chest and hugged her.

She hugged him back. "I do know. Because I'm feeling you inside me, and it's perfect."

No. *She* was perfect. He kissed her again then sat back against the couch. "We're just beginning, angel. Let's go shower and clean up. Then we'll really get started." He nodded at the bag of tricks he'd brought. "I can't wait to show you everything."

· · ·

Ann should have known that nothing would be simple with Jack. As if two mind-blowing orgasms weren't enough, he'd brought toys and product with him. Body butter, some massage oil and lubricant for...easing big things into little things.

For the past two hours, he'd taken his time bathing her, then drying her before massaging her in oil until she wanted to curl around him and sleep for the next ten years. Thank goodness for the blanket she'd thought to put down over her bed or she feared she'd never get the oil—and other stains—out of her sheets.

The sex maniac had gotten hard after giving her a full body massage. She'd grown wet as well, and now he resumed exploring her body. She should have been embarrassed, splayed out on her back on the bed while he stood next to it and rubbed his hands over and in her. But she wasn't. She was still turned on and wanting more.

"You have a big cock." She stared at the thing, knowing Jack had a lot more than six inches.

"It's all about what you do with what you've got, not how much you stuff into your pants." He grinned at her. "But feel free to tell everyone how big I am."

She snorted. "You and that ego."

"Please. What about *your* ego? Don't you like knowing you get me hard?"

"Everything gets you hard."

He frowned. "Not everything. I just happen to have a thing for school teachers and redheads. Oh, and big breasts. Consider yourself warned."

"Jack."

He laughed at her. "Really? *That's* embarrassing? I have my fingers inside you. I've eaten you out, rubbed you all over, and the fact you have large tits is embarrassing?"

"They aren't that big." She was a C-cup, but they fit her frame. Mostly.

"Honey, you have a tiny waist and boobs that fit into my hands. And I have big hands." He spread his fingers wide in front of her face and wiggled them. "You're my personal wet dream come to life."

"Or you're just a really horny guy." She had to keep reminding herself not to fall for his physical charms or slippery tongue. His flattery was going straight to her head.

"You don't want to see it, fine." He didn't look pleased. "Time for some tough love."

"Ah, Jack?"

"Don't worry. You'll thank me for it soon enough. I'm going to sit here, and I want you to lay over my lap. Your ass up, belly down over my legs."

She waited for him to sit up against her headboard, then eased herself into position—to be spanked.

He caressed her ass, and she bit back a moan. Then she noticed a toy in his hand, what looked like a stubby dildo.

"Um, Jack?"

He slapped her butt, hard, and she jerked.

"Stay still. You're a naughty girl, aren't you?" He slapped her again, less hard, but the sting remained. Then he rubbed it away, and heat spread from the slap straight to her clit. Jack must have read her mind, because he fitted a hand between her legs and smiled. "Yeah. You like that. It gets you wet."

He took the small dildo and put it between her legs. "What are you doing?" she asked in a breathless voice.

"Getting your toy wet. This is a butt plug, and it's time I got that ass ready for me."

She swallowed hard. "Will it hurt?"

"Do you want it to?"

She thought about it, amazed at how liberating it felt to be so sexually unrestrained with Jack. Her past boyfriends had never tried anything too kinky with her. Whether due to her being petite and looking innocent or being a schoolteacher, she had no idea.

"Well?" He smacked her ass again.

"A l-little."

"Good." He smiled at her. Never would she have imagined him to be so creative in bed. When they'd been younger, he'd been an amazing lover, but they hadn't done much beyond vanilla sex. Blowjob, missionary, maybe once doggie-style. Jack had surely come into his own since then.

"Okay. Let's try this. No, don't tense up. Easy, angel." He dragged the slender toy out from between her legs and spread her cheeks wide. Then he rimmed her with it. "You like that?"

She was thrusting her ass out, trying to maximize the contact. "Yes."

"Let's give you some more, hmm?" The toy rubbed against the sensitive nerve endings in her ass. Then he pulled it away and drizzled some lube over it. In seconds, he returned to her ass, stroking her and making her long for something more.

When he pushed the tip inside her, she moaned at the flood of sensation bombarding her. Then he moved deeper, and it felt good...until he came to a spot that hurt.

She flinched, and he put a hand on the small of her back. "Easy, angel."

She squirmed. He pulled the toy out, then eased it back in. Small, short thrusts that didn't go past the tight ring that burned. He pulled the toy out and squirted moisture over her anus.

"More lube. Fuck, I want inside you."

She felt his erection under her. The toy returned, but this time it hit that burning spot and continued to slide deeper.

"Push out. That's it. Take it inside," he ordered.

She tried, but it hurt. "Wait."

Jack stopped. "Just feel it."

She let the foreign sensation linger. "Okay."

Slowly, he added a bit more, then pulled the toy out. He thrust it back in, then out, and before she knew it, he was fucking her with it. And she liked it.

"That's it. Oh yeah, that's hot," he rasped. "But there's more."

He moved them both and positioned her so that she was at the edge of the bed, her legs dangling over the edge. She was still belly down, but now he stood between her legs. The plug remained, but Jack tilted her ass up so he could…

"*Jack.*"

"Oh fuck." He inched inside her pussy, the tight fit of his cock in conjunction with the butt plug overwhelming. "That's it. Good girl. Take it." He continued to slide inside her, until both he and the toy filled her. "Oh yeah. Time to submit to your master, angel."

That he was so into the fantasy only enhanced her desire. She had never been so full, and she knew she could experience more. The need for him to move, to take her, made her impatient. "Fuck me."

He slapped her ass, and she cried out with pleasure. He withdrew, then pushed forward again. The slow glide of his body in and out of hers broke any hope of remaining distant from her lover.

She panted as he took her, and his rough handling stirred her to near climax. Then he pushed a button on the plug, and it *vibrated*.

She screamed his name as she came, and he soon joined her, shoving into her so hard they seemed to fuse as one person.

When she could function again, she felt him withdraw. Then he removed the plug, and she felt empty.

"You okay?" he asked and kissed her cheek.

She lay flat, trying to voice an answer. All she could manage was, "Hmmm."

He laughed and kissed her between her shoulder blades. "Good. You stay right there."

Like I'm going anywhere.

He returned to clean her up, the cool damp cloth welcome over her sensitive skin. He turned her over and studied her, his gaze warm, happy. She noticed he'd cleaned himself up, but even flaccid he was imposing. So much muscle and sex appeal in one man. *He should be illegal.*

He tugged her to stand, then whipped the blanket off and tossed it to the floor. "Get in bed."

"Is that an order?"

"You're slurring your words. I exhausted you." He grinned in triumph.

"I just need a break." She yawned. Not a great way to show she could keep up with him. Her excuse was that she hadn't gotten much sleep the last few days, wondering what he'd be like tonight. Though if she'd known to expect a man who'd give her so much pleasure she'd almost pass out, she still wouldn't have gotten much rest.

"Sure thing. Let's lie down so I can get my second wind too."

"Don't you mean third wind?" She laughed at herself and snuggled under the covers. She tensed at first when he joined her, not used to sleeping with a man. But when he spooned her and wrapped a hand around her waist to draw her closer, she sighed and gave in to the need to cuddle.

Life didn't get much better than this.

Chapter Ten

Jack woke with an armful of warm woman pressing her backside into him. She felt right in his arms, and his body agreed. Without thinking about it, he did what felt natural. He slid her leg over his and entered her moist heat.

On their sides, he had no problem taking her. He squeezed her breasts, enthralled with the soft flesh. Still half asleep, afraid he was dreaming, he moved faster, wanting his pleasure before it could disappear.

She moaned and moved with him and dragged his hand from her breast to her clit.

Excited she wanted him as much as he wanted her, he rubbed her until she gave that breathy little cry that signaled she was reaching her peak.

As Ann came around him, he surged one last time and climaxed, filling his lover and wishing he could do it all over again right away. But after his heart stopped racing, he fell back into slumber, pleased to stay connected to her in more ways than one.

When Jack next woke, he was alone.

"Hey, sleepyhead." Ann entered the room holding a cup of steaming coffee. One she sipped from. Not his apparently. She wore a short pink robe that only reached mid-thigh and brought a rosy flush to her skin. Her hair lay in tangles and her blue eyes looked impossibly bright.

He yawned and sat up, gratified when her gaze slipped to his chest and she blushed. The sheets pooled around his waist, covering the part of him already up and offering her a hearty salute.

"Hey yourself." He patted her empty spot next to him. "Come join me." Enchanted by the fairy he desperately wanted to keep, he just stared at her. When she smiled at him with affection in her eyes, his heart dropped at her feet.

She sat next to him, and he took the coffee from her hand. After taking a sip of the super sweet stuff, he grimaced.

She laughed. "It's my coffee, not yours."

"Don't you understand that what's yours is mine?" He put the coffee on the night stand and tackled her to the bed. Looming over her, he licked his lips. "Part your robe. I'm hungry."

She stared at him, her eyes wide, and undid her pink belt, letting the robe open. He leaned down and sucked her nipples until she writhed beneath him.

"If you're hungry," she said between gasps, "I was going to make breakfast... *Oh*."

He'd found what he wanted.

Later, after he'd joined her in an explosive good morning, he smiled down at her. "Breakfast, huh? What did you have in mind? Can't be better than what I just had."

And it wasn't.

He'd planned to take her out to eat, but now sitting at the kitchen table and watching her cook for him was just as good. The domesticity of the scene made him long for more tomorrows waking up next to the sexy redhead—though perhaps cooking classes were in order. "You burned the bacon."

"Because you keep distracting me. Put that thing away." She glared at the erection beneath his jeans.

He grimaced as he adjusted himself. "Damn it. It's not my fault. It's you." And that amazing robe. When she shifted, he saw the swell of her breast and the curve of her ass. So fucking hot, his Ann.

"I can't help being a sex object," she said with a hint of sarcasm.

"Just like I can't help if thinking about you gets me hard. I'm serious," he added when she looked at him with disbelief.

He left his chair and hugged her from behind while she tried to scrape the burned bacon out of the pan. "Even though you can't cook for squat, you are the sweetest thing." *I'm keeping you.*

He felt her laughter. "You already had me. You don't need to butter me up."

"Butter. That's what we need tonight."

She put the bacon down and turned in his arms to face him. "You want *more* sex?"

"Honey, I have you for another twelve hours. You have to do whatever I want." He grinned when she stepped back and looked down his body. "Yeah. I'm good for another few rounds at least."

"Good lord. I don't think I can handle you."

"Sure you can. I'm easy."

She sneered. "That's what they say."

He laughed, because Ann trying to sound mean was just…adorable.

"Come on. Let's eat. I have plans for you."

Plans that included a day spent at the amusement center in town. Among kids and grown-ups alike, they rode the go-carts, played miniature golf and even fit in two frames of bowling. It seemed only fair that he whipped her ass at the games, considering she fried his two remaining brain cells whenever she smiled. Ann had never been an athlete, but hell, when it came to bed sport, she clearly knew how to win him over.

He didn't think she tried to be sexy. She simply *was*.

After they had messed around and had some lunch, he took her to the Fall Festival downtown. Life in Bend hadn't changed much since he'd left. The town still had a festival almost every other weekend. But he enjoyed it, especially watching Ann savor a slice of pumpkin pie in a contest she'd entered. Man, she sure could put away her dessert.

Unfortunately, Riley and Maya were among the contest judges.

"I never win these things," Ann complained while she wiped her chin.

He tried not to smile at the mess she was making.

"Riley's always a judge at these contests, and if I win, she says it will make her appear partial."

"Which is why I wonder why you keep trying," Riley said from behind them. "Besides, you steal my best tricks." She smiled at Ann, but her expression cooled considerably when she noticed him. "Jack."

"Riley." He nodded. Then Maya joined them and the Trio was complete. "Hey, Maya. I saw Dex a few days ago. He said to tell you he said hi."

The woman scowled. Jack hated to admit it, but Ann and her friends could only be classified as dangerous to any man's state of mind. Riley was gorgeous, no question. Maya, scary but no less sexy, made a man think of satin sheets. But Ann… She burned him up, because she was as beautiful on the outside as she was on the inside.

"Excuse us for a minute." Riley latched onto Ann's arm and dragged her away.

Jack turned and saw Anson and Dex approaching. Maya stood her ground next to him, her dark eyes glaring holes into Dex's forehead.

"Hey, Maya." Dex gave her a huge smile, one that seemed to push her buttons.

Anson didn't quite stifle a grin. "Jack."

"Anson."

They both pretended not to notice Maya's hostility, or the way she studied Dex from head to toe, taking in his obvious changes since high school.

"Well, well. If it isn't Bend's own Dexter Black."

Dex didn't even try not to look interested. "Damn, girl. You look good."

"Really? 'You look good'?" She snorted. "That's the best you can do? You might be bigger than you used to be, but you're still just as lame." She turned on her heel and left.

Dex stared after her and sighed. "That is one fine ass."

"Attached to one pissed off woman. She'd sooner punch you than date you, dumbass." Anson cuffed his cousin in the back of the head.

"Oh, you're one to talk. I saw Riley hotfooting it away. Guess your plan to annoy her into your bed isn't working."

Anson shoved Dex, and Dex shoved back. Jack would have stepped in except the bravado and trash talk amused him. Then they turned on him.

"So, Jack" Anson said. "You and Ann."

Dex nodded. "They looked pretty chummy to me the other night at dinner."

"I don't kiss and tell. But then, I don't have to." Jack smiled.

"Asshole." Anson sighed. "At least she's nice. Riley is a huge pain in my ass."

"You mean you'd like her to be," Dex murmured.

"Shut it. Just because it's obvious to the rest of the world how much you want inside Maya's pants does not mean I'm mooning over Riley. I'm trying to be friendly while building a solid business. But the woman is colder than ice."

"Uh huh." Even Jack didn't believe that one.

"I know, right? He thinks we're stupid." Dex laughed. "Cousin, if you're not trying to win the woman over, why did you move your business right next door to hers? Why send her bouquets of flowers?"

"Really? Flowers?"

Anson flushed. "He's talking shit."

"Am I?"

"I need a drink." Anson shoved his cousin once again and stalked away.

Dex smiled. "It's fun watching him flounder. Everything's always come a little too easy to him. But not Riley."

"Don't they hate each other?"

"She hates him for sure. Anson feels anything but for his chocolate goddess."

Jack coughed. Not exactly a PC thing to say. "If she hears you call her that, she'll kill you."

"I used to call her that back in high school and she liked it. Remember? She made the best chocolate chip brownies ever."

"Oh yeah." Speaking of which, he wondered if she'd make some for him to take on a picnic with his redhead.

Riley returned with Ann, who was all smiles.

"My chocolate goddess." Dex beamed at her.

Riley tried to be stern, but Jack saw a grin break through. "You big goofball. Aside from pissing off Maya, how are you?"

Dex swung Riley into a huge hug. "How is it you keep getting prettier? Your skin is flawless. Gorgeous. Look at the play of shadow over you. When can I shoot you?"

"Excuse me?" Ann arched a brow.

Jack slung an arm around her shoulders. "I'm assuming he means with a camera."

"Huh? Of course." Dex shook his head. "Academics. Am I right?"

Riley snickered. "Teachers in *lurveee*."

Ann blushed.

Jack only smiled, and Riley's eyes grew wider.

Dex glanced from him to Riley. "What?"

"Nothing. Look, I gotta go. I have to find Maya before she gets a gun and shoots you. As in, not with a camera."

Dex sighed. "Still mad about the prom, huh? She swore she'd get even with me."

"You know Maya. She holds a grudge."

"Yeah, but she's so pretty while being mad. I forgive her."

Even Ann smiled at the charmer.

Jack didn't like that. "Okay, we're out of here." He leaned down and whispered to her, "I have five more hours."

"Geesh. Going to count down to the last second, eh?"

"You got it."

Jack said his goodbyes before dragging Ann away with him.

"I wanted to hang with Riley."

"Well, I want you all to myself. Unless you'd rather blow me right—"

She slapped a hand over his mouth.

"Jackson Samuel Bloom, watch your mouth."

He laughed and licked her palm. She wiped her hand on his jacket, muttering under her breath. Then she grabbed him and yanked him with her to the car.

As he drove them back to her house, he wondered about something. "You don't care if I drive, do you?"

"Why would I?" She seemed puzzled.

"Some women would see me driving as a statement of control."

"You do have five more hours. Then…payback." She smirked at him.

"So if there was no bet, just you and me hanging out, would you want to drive?"

"Would you care if I did?"

He thought about it. "No. You're a good driver."

She nodded. "There's your answer. You've never been sexist or racist as long as I've known you. You've never treated Maya or Riley different, which is more than I can say for half the school. And you've never acted like having a smart girlfriend was a crime."

"I love smart women." One smart woman in particular.

"You always treated me with respect." She frowned. "Well, almost always."

He didn't want to talk about the past. "Now, today, do you feel good being with me?"

"Yeah, I guess." She looked out the window as she asked, "You like being with me, don't you?"

"Yes. And not just for the sex. That's amazing, don't get me wrong, but I like you a lot, Ann." He decided to push. "I'd like us to keep seeing each other. After the bet."

"Seeing each other."

"You know. Dating. Boyfriend-girlfriend. Being exclusive."

"Oh."

They drove the next few minutes in silence. He was dying to know what she thought about his idea.

Once inside, she turned to him. "What do I get out of it?"

"Excuse me?" He hung up their coats, straightening out the sleeves so the jackets were even, then noticed her surprised expression. "What?"

"Nothing." But he saw the smile she tried to hide.

"What? Spit it out, Weaver."

She grinned. "I just think it's cute that you're a neat

freak."

"Oh." He glanced at the closet, and she laughed. Having her in a good mood, he took advantage. "So you and me. Us." She stopped laughing and backed away as he advanced. Finally, she took him seriously. "What do you think?"

She stopped moving when she backed into the wall. He stood over her, feeling like a conquering hero and loving it. He freely admitted he got off on being in command, but only because he knew she was as strong as he was, and she *let* him take charge. He needed that trust from her. Maybe, once he felt sure of her feelings, they could revisit the past and clear the air. But right now he needed a hold on the woman.

He hated to keep resorting to sex, but it seemed to work. She softened after he pleasured her.

Jack put a hand around her neck. Gently, but he kept her right where he wanted her. Judging from the increase in her breathing and dilation of her pupils, she liked his hand right where it was.

"You and me, Ann."

He used his other hand to unbutton her blouse. He slipped his hand inside and past her bra to tease her nipples.

"You're cheating," she moaned.

He loved that she knew he intended to manipulate her with sex yet couldn't help herself. "I'll do anything to get you." *And keep you.* "Come on, Ann. What could it hurt?" As soon as he said the words, he knew he'd made a mistake. Her eyes darkened with memory.

He didn't want her lingering on their past mistakes. He wanted her looking toward a better future. So he pinched her nipple and kissed her. His hand on her neck remained, but he didn't tighten it. Restraining her served to heighten her desire. And before he knew it, the minx had opened his jeans and had her hands on him.

"Ann. *Fuck.*"

"If I say yes, what does that mean?" She stroked him, rubbing her thumb over his cockhead.

He widened his stance, mentally begging her to cup his balls, to drop to her knees and suck him off. That was an image he wanted to commit to memory.

"I—ah—it means… You… God, Ann." He moaned and started humping her hand. "You and me, angel. Just us. No one else."

"No cheating," she clarified. "I'd have to trust you."

"And I'd have to trust you," he added and nearly came when she squeezed him.

"I'll think about it. That's the best I can do right now."

"I'll prove it to you. We can make it work." His heart lightened with hope while his cock hardened with lust. "Now on your knees." He checked his watch, barely able to focus. "I have four hours and twenty-six minutes left to boss you around." Though right now he wasn't sure who was bossing whom.

She dropped to her knees, pulled his pants and underwear down, then drew his thick shaft to her lips. She stared up at him as her tongue darted out to lick his slit.

"Shit. Ann. Oh God."

She smiled and watched him watching her. Then she took the crown of his cock between her lips and sucked. "Hmm." She bobbed over him, and their gazes locked.

He wondered what she saw as she sent him spiraling in pleasure. It didn't take him long before he reached his end. He shouted her name and clutched her head as he spent, and she swallowed him down.

"Best. Girlfriend. Ever," he said between breaths.

She grinned and licked him up, then rose to her feet. "That was sixty seconds well spent."

He might have been more upset about the jibe if he could get his brain to function.

She laughed. "I swear your eyes nearly rolled up in your head. You have a sexy O-face."

"Shut up."

"Oh, he's blushing," she teased. "Seriously. I bet you could make real money in amateur home movies. You know what I'm talking about. Quit your day job and show some skin for sin." She wiggled her brows.

"Ann Weaver." He feigned shock as he tucked himself back into his pants. "I can't believe you even know what P-O-R-N is!"

Her own cheeks burned red, and he laughed. "You should see your own O-face. I'm game. Let's film it."

"No way. Uh-uh. I'm a *teacher*."

"With a sexy-as-hell body and the ability to make me come in less than a minute. I'm a teacher too, but I can admit to liking sex."

"Liking it is just fine. Filming it? No."

He pulled her in for a hug and a kiss. "I was kidding, Ms. Stick-in-the-Mud."

"Stick in the—"

"Four hours and eighteen minutes to go," he said checking his watch. Then he smacked her ass. "Now go get naked and spread out on the bed. We're far from done, wench."

"That's Ms. Weaver to you."

"Oh, the naughty schoolboy and his teacher. Good one. That's what we'll do next."

Ann pretended shock, but the pretty red staining her cheeks showed she was more than interested.

Oh yeah. He had it bad for teacher. *Real* bad.

Chapter Eleven

Figuring Jack would want some space on Sunday after spending almost every second of their weekend together, Ann mentioned he might want to leave so she could do some household chores.

Jack sat at the kitchen table, sipping his coffee. "I'm good. So what chores do we have to do?"

"*We?*"

"Sure. I figure if I help you dust, you can help me figure out what to get Julie for the surprise party my mother is planning. You know, to celebrate the new baby."

She stared at him. "You want *my* help? I don't really know Julie. Why not ask Dan?" She felt silly, but shopping together felt as if they were taking their relationship to the next level. They were already having sex. He wanted them to call each other boyfriend and girlfriend. Then what? Move in together? Get engaged? What about her grand plans for revenge? Not easy to finish if she fell in love with the guy.

His thoughtfulness toward his sister-in-law wasn't helping her resolve, either.

Great going with that, Ann. Why don't you sleep with him again *to prove how over him you are?* She could almost hear Maya's scathing voice ripping her a new one.

"Ann?"

She shook herself. "What? Oh. I guess. I need to clean up the kitchen, dust and pick up the living room. You know, house stuff. And I definitely need a shower."

"You can clean the shower and yourself at the same time. That's how I do it." He looked around, no doubt noting the mess of dishes in the drying rack, a few in the sink and the random assortment of cans and boxes of macaroni she hadn't gotten around to organizing yet.

She grinned, feeling a little more on even keel. "You have issues, you know that?"

"I don't follow."

She pulled out a chair and sat next to him. "It's kind of cute, your addiction to cleanliness."

"I wouldn't say I'm addicted." He concentrated on his coffee, taking small sips.

"I would. Maybe it's an OCD thing."

His cheeks turned red. "Shut up."

"Look at you. All embarrassed because you and Mr. Clean are in a monogamous relationship."

"You know, you're a lot prettier when that mouth is occupied with other things." His smirk made *her* blush.

"Fine. I'll get the cleaning stuff."

He actually hummed while he dusted. She wouldn't have believed it if she hadn't seen and heard it herself. He seemed to enjoy cleaning up while she put the groceries away and straightened up the dishes.

After a while, she realized the house had grown quiet. She tracked him down in her bedroom, straightening up her clothes.

He noticed her and raised a brow. "What? We made a

mess in here."

"Oh? You're wearing your mess. That's my stuff on the floor." After her harried week, she'd foregone being neat. Normally she put things away, but this side of Jack intrigued her. Seeing him so domestic made him seem more real. More human. More...

She stopped him when he grabbed her laundry basket. "Okay, that's enough. Go watch TV or read a book. I'm going to shower."

"But I could—"

"You are *not* washing my dirty clothes." Gross *and* embarrassing. "Go downstairs. I'll shower, then we can go get Julie something."

He brightened. "Actually, I think I'll head home for some fresh clothes. I'll be back in half an hour."

"Okay."

He kissed her, pulling her in for that familiar, unmistakable warmth that she knew would be her undoing. Being with Jack was starting to become the norm. She liked it, liked him, more than she should.

He moved away with a sigh. "You know, there's no rush. Why don't we..." He nodded back to the bed.

"Nope. We hit the sheets, we'll be there all day. We're shopping, remember?"

"Fine." He turned to leave, and she swore she heard, *"I'll get you later."*

Once alone in the shower, she tried to wash away her concerns. Easier said than done. The soap suds swirled around the drain, but her confusion still remained.

She'd thought she was doing the right thing by getting herself together, confronting the past—in particular, Jack. But she didn't want to revisit the pain of old mistakes. She wanted to take charge of her life and put her troubles far behind her. But it seemed as if Jack planned to make her a part of his future.

And maybe she wanted that too.

Confusing sex with love. A familiar pattern. Remember, he dumped you once. What's to say he won't do it again?

After finishing her shower, she dried and dressed. She planned on putting a bit of distance between her and Jack, though she didn't intend to tell him that. The sex between them was new, and sure, they'd always been good together. But the rest, the dating, the sharing, that took its toll. A few more days in his company and she was pretty sure she'd be ready to say goodbye. He'd no doubt act like an ass soon enough.

One could hope.

Jack returned when he said he would. They decided to walk downtown, a short trip into the heart of Bend. There they perused each store—even the ones that had nothing to do with a baby. Testing him, Ann tried to bore him to death by shopping for hours, and not just for Julie, but for herself as well. Her excuse being she rarely took the time to go shopping.

She hadn't expected him to like being with her *that* much.

"No, I like the blue one better."

She turned to see him eyeing the dress she'd tried on, as she looked at herself in front of the store mirror. "Really? You like this better than the pink one?"

"Brings out the blue in your eyes." He winked.

To her astonishment, he wasn't joking around or mildly tolerating her, but offering what appeared to be a sincere opinion.

"You're having fun, aren't you?"

He laughed. "Yeah. Why not? If I wasn't out shopping with you, I'd be working on something for Dr. Singer or hiking at Todd Lake. And after our trip last week, hiking turns me on. Not cool when you're by yourself in the woods and end up passing curious hikers, let me tell you."

Her cheeks felt warm. "Oh, um. Okay." She hurried into the dressing room to put her own clothes back on. Then she took the dresses she'd tried on and placed them on the return rack.

"You're not going to get it?" he asked.

"Nah. Just window shopping." On her salary, she needed to be bowled over to splurge on clothes. Though she loved the dress, she didn't love the price tag.

Jack plucked the dress off the rack and took it to the counter.

"What are you doing?"

"Buying you this dress." He noted a pair of earrings near the counter that she'd coveted earlier. "Those too."

"Jack."

The saleswoman smiled and added them to the purchase. "Good choice." She rang up the sale and handed Jack the bag. He grabbed it and Ann's hand and left the store.

"Where to next?"

She felt awkward, both pleased and weirded out that he'd purchased her something. Especially considering her conflicted feelings for him. Then another thought hit her, this one mortifying.

"You didn't have to buy me anything." She tilted her chin up. "I can afford it, you know."

He sighed. "This isn't going to be a big deal, is it? It's just a dress."

"And earrings."

"So? I plan to strip the dress off you at some point. It's more a present for me, really." He nodded to more stores. "Now, where to next?"

She gave in and took him to a baby store, where they selected a stuffed owl and some neutral-colored onesies for the baby.

"Do you think Julie will want to learn the baby's sex?" she asked as they left.

"Probably. Julie likes to know what's what. Dan too."

They hit a bistro for lunch and ordered sandwiches and drinks. Jack insisted on paying, despite her protests, and then they took their seats while they waited for their order to appear.

"I could have paid," she said.

"Look, it's my weekend. I'm in charge."

"You lost your authority hours ago," she reminded him.

"I know. So you should ease me back into being a normal guy by letting me do whatever I want."

"I should, hmm?" She was such a sucker for that bright blue joy in his eyes. When he grew so animated and happy, she had a hard time refusing him anything.

"Yeah." He sipped from his drink, watching her. "So…"

"Go ahead. Say what's on your small, male mind."

He laughed with her. "You're so funny when you're insulting. And everything about you is pretty."

"Jack, stop. I'll get a big ego if you keep flattering me."

"Nah. You'll shrug it off, like you do all my compliments." He studied her from the top of her head to her toes hidden under the table. "Yep. I like the whole package."

Unfortunately, she really liked him too. What to do about that?

"You had a point?" she prodded.

"Julie's pregnant with her second. My mom's on me to settle down, but I keep telling her I don't have time. What about you? Ever thought about kids?"

She shrugged, keeping it casual and not trying to read too much into that segue. "Sure. I always figured I'd be a mom someday. But I'm only…" She did the math and felt her biological clock start ticking. "Well, I'll be thirty next year."

"Still young." He nodded. "You have plenty of time to

start a family."

"I'd like to do it the old fashioned way. I know too many single moms having a hard time. I'd prefer to get married first. Then again, I'm sure my single friends did too." She sighed. "It's scary. Relationships don't last anymore." She looked at him, uncomfortable at the intensity in his eyes. "What?"

"So you're off marriage altogether? Scared it will go bad so you quit the market?"

"I didn't say that. It's just... I need to take my time and not rush things. I don't see a ring on *your* finger." She stared pointedly at his bare left hand.

"True. But I'm not against marriage. I'd like to get married someday, have kids and a house."

Her heart raced. "Oh? Ever proposed to anyone?"

"No." He stared at her. "The one I wanted got away a long time ago."

Did he mean her or some other woman from his past? As much as she wanted to know, she didn't want to spoil the day either way. "Right. Well, enough of this marriage talk. Why don't you tell me about your job?"

"My job?"

A server brought over their sandwiches. As they ate, Jack described his role as an environmental engineer at the college in detail. It seemed he had a terrific job that satisfied him.

"We're both teachers," he said as he pushed away his empty plate. "Tell me what it's like being around so many little kids every day. I love Josh, but he's a handful. How do you manage a room full of them?"

She smiled. "I love children. They're so innocent, so full of ideas and so much fun. To see them learn and get excited about knowledge is fantastic. And yes, I have to have a lot of patience, but I'm doing what I love. What could be better than that?"

"You're going to be such a great mother."

She started. "Ah, thanks."

"I mean, imagine a little girl with your looks and intelligence. She'll have all the boys wrapped around her little finger." He smiled, and the soft look he gave her raised her blood pressure. "She'll need a big strong daddy to keep the boys in line."

"You have babies on the brain, don't you?"

He chuckled and lost his faraway look, thank God. Because if he'd suggested it, she might have been stupid enough to try making a few rug-rats *right now*. Totally not on her agenda, nor should it be with *him*.

"Blame my mother," he said while she gathered her scattered thoughts. "She's been going on and on about Dan and Julie, about my pathetic love life and how she's might die before she sees grandchildren from me."

"Wow. She's really working the guilts."

"That's Mom." He shook his head. "But I love her. Your parents leaving you alone about grandkids?"

"Well, my mom is always interested in my love life. Other than that, they've been mostly quiet."

"Love life, hmm?" He dragged a finger over her cheek. "What other men do I have to worry about? You hiding a stash of lovers?" He sounded lighthearted, but a glint in his eyes had her wondering.

"Yeah, I have a whole harem of pool boys waiting on me at home."

He relaxed. "I see. Guess I'd better up my game then. How about ice cream?"

"Ugh. I'm full." And too jittery around him to eat. He made her nervous. She kept thinking about future babies and rings and a life with him, which only served to show she hadn't learned jack—literally—from her mistakes in high school. "Besides, if I keep eating, I'll blow up like a balloon."

"Fine. You can help me eat mine. I have a hankering for

mint chocolate chip."

Her favorite. Did the man forget anything? "You suck."

"Yeah, I do." He wiggled his brows, and once again she recalled how they'd spent last night. She hoped she didn't look as red as she felt as they left for the ice cream shop.

Because they had to walk home, by the time they'd reached her place, she didn't feel guilty for helping him finish his ice cream.

"Well, it's been a fun day." She walked up the steps and paused at the front door when he latched onto her arm.

"Hell no. We're not done, angel."

She tingled at the endearment. "We're not?"

"You have to try on that dress for me. Come on. Please?"

Recalling his plans to take it off her, she frowned. "No funny business. I'll try it on, but you have to go after. I can't be walking funny at school tomorrow. The kids will talk."

He grinned. "Yes, Ms. Weaver."

"If you were in my class, I have no doubt you'd be at the naughty desk all year long."

He laughed and followed her inside.

She pointed to the couch, not trusting him or herself together in her bedroom. "You stay here."

"Spoilsport."

She took her bag with her into the bedroom and tried on the dress. She had to take off her bra to wear it, but the dress had its own support. She smoothed it out as she looked in the mirror. It looked terrific. She added the earrings, touched to know he'd bought them for her.

Then she added a pair of blue heels from her closet and knew she'd have to wear this out somewhere soon. Before it grew too cold to be comfortable.

"Okay. Here it is." She walked into the living room and rounded the couch to face Jack.

He just stared. "You look amazing."

"Thanks."

"Twirl around. Let me see the back."

She felt like a million bucks in the knee-length silky material. The dress flattered her curves while giving her body more oomph. She didn't feel tiny in it either. She felt like a sexy man-eater. Especially the way Jack looked at her.

With her back to him, she glanced over her shoulder for his reaction.

Jack's smile was wicked. He scooted forward on the couch and pulled her back by the hips to stand closer to him. Then he ran his hands up her legs.

She shivered. "Jack?"

He reached her waist under the dress and tugged her panties down.

"What are you doing?"

"What does it feel like?" came the low pitched answer.

Her panties continued down her legs and pooled at her feet.

"Step out of them," he ordered.

She had a hard time breathing past the excitement filling her from head to toe and centering between her legs. "I thought I said no funny business." She stepped out of the panties and turned to face him.

"Angel, there's nothing funny about how hard I'm gonna fuck you right now. Does this make you want to laugh?" He thrust a hand between her legs and slid through her arousal. "Hot and wet. My two favorite words."

She strangled on a laugh that shifted into a moan as he pumped a finger inside her. "Jack…"

"Yes, sweetheart. I'll make it all better."

Chapter Twelve

Jack couldn't think straight as he let her envelop his finger. So hard he could split wood, his cock demanded a taste of what his fingers felt—a warm, tight welcome.

He'd known where this afternoon was heading all damn day. Waking with her this morning had felt more than right. But the true test of where their future was heading had been this afternoon. Shopping with a woman, including any of exes and even his mother, was normally akin to torture. But being with Ann all day had been nothing but fun. He loved seeing the excitement light up her face when she saw something she liked.

He'd also had a feeling she'd been testing him, trying to pull away from him emotionally. If he hadn't been so tuned in to the woman, he might have missed it. But he'd noticed and taken steps.

She couldn't leave him behind. Not now. Now when they'd just started to reconnect. They would learn as they went along, but one thing he'd never take for granted—the heat they generated between them.

He'd only ever felt its like with Ann, and God knew he'd tried to bond with other women since their breakup. But no one had ever gotten to him on both an emotional and physical level like Ann Weaver.

Her breathing grew choppy. She clutched his shoulders and stared down at him while he played with her pussy.

"You feel good, baby." So good he wanted her to sink over him and ride him until he came. Nothing beat an orgasm buried in that hot little body. He loved her mouth, but her pussy had him in heaven in no time.

That thought in mind, he pushed her dress up, loving the smooth touch of the material, especially how it hugged her soft skin. "Hold this for me," he ordered.

She gripped the dress, and he focused on her pussy. Widening her stance, he nudged her folds apart and began to kiss her there, satisfied by her low moan. She tasted so sweet, and knowing how much this pleased her gave him a rush like no other.

He sucked and kissed her, thrusting his finger faster. Her breathy cries and moans sounded like music, and he wanted more. He pulled back and stared up at her, seeing the lust on her face. An angel drawn to sin...by him.

With a pained grimace, he stood. "Unzip me and take me out."

She unfastened his jeans with shaky fingers. "God, I want you."

Words he loved to hear. "Me too. Take off that dress. Slowly."

She stepped back and inched the dress up over her. She slipped it over her hips, gliding the material over her belly, her breasts. Then she let it roll over her shoulders and tossed it aside. Wearing nothing but heels, she stood before him—proud, sexy and unafraid.

"Christ." He leaned down to take a firm nipple in his

mouth while he played with her breasts. He had her writhing under his touch, a firm hold that demanded her obedience. Since fantasies of domination seemed to appeal to both of them, he put his hand at her neck and squeezed lightly. "Who do you belong to?"

Her blue eyes seemed impossibly dark as she answered, "You."

"You, *Sir*," he added to amp the kink.

"You, Sir," she repeated.

He gave her nipple a tiny pinch and saw her start. "I can do whatever I want because I own you, don't I?"

A strange emotion crossed her face, then disappeared just as fast, making him wonder what he'd seen. "Yes, Sir. Please fuck me, Sir."

With his fingers around her neck, he used his hold on her to pull her behind the couch and bend her over. "Stay like that. Right there."

"Yes, Sir."

He slapped her ass, and she cried out.

"Ask me for another." Fuck, he was close to coming. He loved playing games with Ann—she looked so innocent yet got off on being so dirty. His woman, for sure.

"Please, Sir. Spank me again."

"Yes, angel. You need it." He spanked her twice more, then couldn't wait any longer. Positioning himself behind her, he guided himself to her pussy and thrust hard, gliding through her wet passage.

Like coming home.

He felt her grip him as she cried out, coming around him while he rode through to his own orgasm. Emptying inside Ann added to the feelings of dominance and possession. Total Neanderthal bullshit, but he didn't care. He fucked her until his knees felt shaky and he grew lightheaded.

Spent, he withdrew and saw her red ass cheeks and the

mess he'd left, and couldn't be happier.

"See? No funny business, Ann. I promise."

"You're a dick, you know that?" Her voice was muffled by the couch and the hair over her face. She straightened and made a dash for the bedroom.

Feeling like a total stud, he cleaned himself up and waited for her to rejoin him. He'd had a sexual marathon of a weekend with his *girlfriend*. What more could a man want?

An image of Ann, pregnant, filled his mind's eye. He wanted to be more uncomfortable at the thought, but he wasn't. What the hell did that mean? Had his mother's urgings and Julie's pregnancy brainwashed him into wanting a kid? Or was it his own longings, a second chance with Ann and a future together, finally coming to the fore?

Ann returned wearing baggy sweats. Even so, she looked adorable. Her cheeks were flushed and her eyes sparkled with anger.

"What now?" he asked, happy and not at all repentant.

"You knew what I meant about no funny business."

"You could have said no." And he'd have stopped, even if it killed him.

Her red cheeks gratified him. "Yeah, well, I have no willpower when it comes to you. I swear, I have more dirty underwear than I know what to do with."

"I could always wash your—"

"*No.* Now get out. Go get ready for your workweek while I try to decompress from mine." She added under her breath, "I wouldn't be surprised if your dick falls off from overuse."

He laughed as she pushed him out the door, always amused whenever innocent-looking Ann Weaver, second grade teacher, swore like a truck driver.

• • •

The rest of the night passed by in a blur. Work went smoothly the next day, and he and Ann met Monday night at a coffee shop for a walk around the neighborhood.

He loved that she liked to be physical both in bed and outside it. Walking, hiking, even biking, though she'd made it clear she didn't particularly care for running, Ann enjoyed the outdoors, like him. He'd been with too many women who only wanted to watch movies or sit on the computer, Facebooking their way through life.

They took their coffees to go and bundled up as they walked under the fading twilight. He could see her clearly under the full moon, growing brighter as the clouds dispersed. Nearby, others walked along the sidewalks, enjoying the outside air as well.

"Good day?" she asked.

He wanted to hear that every day. He'd come home from work and see her waiting for him. In the kitchen, the living room, by the front door. She'd smile and welcome him home. They'd kiss, and she'd ask about his day, just like that. Then he'd ask about hers. They'd share stories and decide what to do for dinner.

The domestic scene would have bored him a few years ago, but lately he couldn't think of anything but being closer to Ann.

"Hello? Earth to Jack?"

He hid a grin behind his coffee cup. "Yeah, I'm settling in at the college. How about you? Any more Grand Canyons to deal with?"

She laughed. "Not yet. Though I did interrupt a glue fight and had to send Mike and Toby to the principal. Those two have gotten pretty bad."

After talking and walking some more, they fell into a nice, peaceful quiet. Birds still chirped, and the occasional bat swooped over head, looking for insects to eat between the tall pines that surrounded them.

The neighborhood suited her. Him too.

"I was thinking," Ann said quietly.

"Oh?" He wondered if she'd want to keep her house. Maybe they could move in together somewhere bigger? Though he planned on renting something small first, like the cottage he'd been inquiring about around the corner from her place, investing in property while in a buyer's market made sense.

"We're moving too fast."

Something with a garden, because she liked to—"What?"

"It's just… We're spending all our time together, having a lot of sex," she said in a lower voice, "and I'm afraid this is all too soon."

"What's too soon? The fact we like being together?" *Fuck*. He'd pushed too hard. But they had a good thing going. Was he wrong to want more?

"No. But being boyfriend and girlfriend… I just don't know that I'm ready to commit to that. You've only been back two weeks. "

"I know. But, Ann, we've known each other forever. Being back with you feels like I never left."

"But you *did* leave." She gave him a hard glare. "There's a lot of life that went on between then and now. I don't think it's wrong for me to want to take some time to think about it."

Though hurt and annoyed, he forced himself to be cool. "I thought we liked hanging out together. Or was that just me?"

She blew out a breath. "No. I like being with you. But I'm used to being on my own or having girl time with Riley and Maya. Now there's you, and—"

"And what? We're having sex and it's amazing. There's a problem with that?"

She turned beet red. "Would you *please* keep your voice

down?"

"Sorry." He wanted to punch something. "Is it the sex? Too kinky?" Had he misread the signals? Had he confused his pleasure for hers? At the thought, he felt sick.

"Would you *shush*?" She slapped a hand over his mouth and tugged him with her out of the path of an oncoming couple and their kids. "No. The sex is fine. Amazing. Orgasmic. Every time." She frowned. "But that's not normal. I mean, sure, it had been a while for me before you. But even then I never came *every* time." She huffed. "That's not the point."

Relieved he hadn't screwed that up at least, he tried to hear her out. "So what, then?"

She looked around, then up at him. "I...we..."

He had a feeling he knew what she wanted to say. They'd never talked about the past. He'd been hoping not to bring that up until she was so in lust and in love with him she wouldn't care what he said. Thinking about his inadequacies and her betrayal hurt all over again.

"Fuck, Ann. Just say it."

She scowled. "It's too soon. You just blew back into town. For all I know you could be playing me."

"Are you serious?" He gaped. "Playing you? For what? Why?"

She bit her lower lip and looked away. "You're a guy aren't you? That's what guys do."

She couldn't mean him and high school. She'd started that. Had someone hurt her since then? She was right. He didn't know her as well as he might wish. "Ann, I'd never do that. I am what you see. I know it's been years, but I'm here now, and I plan to stay." *Go slow, dumb ass. Don't scare her off. Take your time.* "Look, I'm sorry if I pushed, okay? I feel like I know you since we had something deep between us before, but you're right. That was a long time ago. We're lovers now, and I don't want that to end. We'll take it slow, however slow you want. Okay?"

She didn't look as happy as he'd thought she might. "Okay." She pasted a smile on her face. "Thanks. I appreciate you hearing me out."

"I'll always listen. One thing I've been told I do well."

"That's not the only thing." She sighed. "You really worked me hard this weekend."

He had to chuckle at her woebegone tone. "But it was worth it, wasn't it?"

She glanced up at him and gave a true smile. "Yeah."

• • •

Ann finished the walk with him feeling better about things. Getting that pressing relationship off her back had made a world of difference. She didn't feel so guilty about liking the new him and still loathing the old Jack. Some meaningless sex didn't commit his feelings or hers.

But back at home and in bed, she had to raise the bullshit flag. No matter how she prettied it up or tried to pretend one of them wouldn't be hurt at the end of it all, she knew she'd have a hard time separating herself from Jack when it ended.

He'd burrowed himself under her skin, despite how hard she'd tried not to let him. Those dimples, his big blue eyes, his easy charm.

Why couldn't he have been a complete ass while shopping? Or after she'd slowed things down tonight? He could have had a mantrum, as Maya liked to call them. Getting all pissy and demanding rights because he'd given her a few orgasms.

Orgasm—a bland word for the incredible joy and selflessness he'd demonstrated while giving her pleasure.

She shivered just thinking about how he used his mouth, his hands, his amazing tongue…

Too exhausted to do more than fall into a restless night

dreaming about him, she woke the next morning and knew it would be a long day.

It was.

Andrew and Jane picked fights with the other kids. Her headache brewed, and the teacher's lounge had run out of her favorite creamer, forcing her to drink her coffee black. Totally gross. Then she'd returned to a super clean house, reminding her of how sweet and funny Jack had been with his cleanliness issues. Such a nice guy on the one hand, and a kinky lover on the other. She found it difficult to reconcile him with the boy who'd treated her so shabbily long ago. Because he'd started out like this nice Jack, the loving, kind-hearted soul who put her needs first and treated her like gold.

And then he'd disappeared, replaced by an asshole who'd broken her heart. Was that asshole still lurking down there somewhere?

She'd grown up a lot since then, but she'd never been able to understand why he'd dumped her like that. The time had come to talk to him about it, yet she was loath to break their fragile peace. Especially after last night's talk.

The school day ended, and she went home with a heavy heart. Happy, sad, and every conflicted feeling in between. Jack called and, as usual, her heart raced.

She answered her cell and fell into her couch, letting it swallow her up. "Hello?" She sighed.

"Bad day?" he asked.

"That obvious?"

"I know your sighs, and that one usually involves a headache, a problem or someone stealing your chocolate."

She smiled despite herself. "Perceptive."

"Tell me all about it."

I think I might be falling for you, and I'm afraid. "I ran out of creamer. My kids were monsters. And— Hold on, another call." She didn't recognize the number, but it was a local area code.

"Sure."

She put him on hold and answered the other line. "Hello?"

"Oh, is this Ann Weaver?"

The voice sounded familiar, but she couldn't place it. "Yes."

"Hi, Ann. This is Laura Bloom, Josh's grandmother. Jack's mom."

"Oh yes, Mrs. Bloom. Hi, how are you?" *I have your son on the other line. And by the way, I can't stop thinking about him going down on me,* she thought with a touch of hysteria, as if those words might actually pop out.

"Call me Laura, honey. I was calling to invite you to my daughter-in-law's surprise party. She's pregnant, and we're so excited to be adding another one to the family."

"Congratulations." She paused. "But, Laura, I don't know Julie or Dan that well outside of school and Josh."

"I know, but since you're so close to Jack, I thought it might be nice if all us girls had some time to ourselves."

She swallowed a groan. "Th-that would be lovely. But my schedule is kind of full, especially with the school Halloween party, and I—"

"A lot of folks are busy this time of year. So I took that into account. The party isn't until next month. On a Saturday. I'll shoot you an invitation with the exact time and date. It would mean so much to Julie if you could be there."

How to say no to that?

"Um, sure. Okay. Thanks for inviting me."

"Wonderful!" Laura chatted a moment more, then hung up.

Ann realized she'd left Jack on hold. She hurried to catch the call. "Sorry. Are you there?"

"Fell asleep waiting, but yeah."

She groaned. "That was your mother." A perfect end to

her less-than-stellar day.

"What?"

"She just invited me to Julie's surprise party."

"Oh. Are you going?"

"Yes. She guilted me into it."

She didn't get any sympathy from Jack. "Ha. She did the same to me. She's a real piece of work, all right," he teased. "Look, don't worry about it. I can make some excuse to get you out of going."

Ann felt worse, because he was being so nice. What had Julie done to deserve her indifference, anyway? Nothing. Ann loved Josh, so why not be supportive? "No, no. I want to go."

"You do?"

"It'll be fun. As long as your mother doesn't grill me about you."

"I'll make sure she doesn't. And I'll be there, so I can protect you, my small, feeble lady."

"Ha ha. Very funny."

"I thought so." She sensed him grin through the phone. "Anyway, I called to say hi, and to invite you to dinner with Dan, Julie and my folks on Thursday."

"Good timing."

"In light of Mom's invite, I'd say so. You should come. They're a fun couple. My brother was a pain growing up, but he turned into an okay guy."

She knew how close the family was. It was something she envied.

"And, Ann, no pressure on you to be anything but yourself with me and them," he said quietly. "No girlfriend bullshit, I promise. Just fun between friends, who happen to be lovers."

Why, why, WHY can't you be an asshole? "Sure. It'll be fun."

"Great. Talk to you later. I have to go. Anson and I are hitting the gym."

"Sounds like a great time—not."

He laughed and hung up.

She sat there, staring at her cell phone, wondering why she couldn't stop herself from growing closer to the man she knew she should be running far, far away from.

Chapter Thirteen

Ann sighed. Hello hump day. Another school day ended as the bell rang. She still hadn't resolved her feelings on committing to exclusively dating Jack yet, which bothered the heck out of her because she had a bad feeling she'd fallen in love with him all over again. In retrospect, their weekend together had been beyond magical. Even their argument Monday night had ended in her favor, and he'd given her space last night.

As a result, she both looked forward to and dreaded Thursday night dinner. She wanted to be with Jack again, to see him smile with his family. But would they consider her and Jack a *couple?* And would that push Jack to pressure her to commit again?

She still didn't think she was ready for that.

"Hey, Ann." Trey Atwood popped into her classroom after a brief knock. "We still on for tonight?"

She blanked. "Tonight?"

His smile dropped. "For the movie?"

She suddenly recalled the email he'd sent her last week. About the movie she'd agreed to see with him...before she and Jack had gotten so hot and heavy. *Crap*.

She felt obligated to go with Trey, yet she also felt dishonest about the date. But why should she? She and Jack hadn't committed to each other—well, she hadn't anyway. A movie was just a movie.

"Sorry. I spaced. I thought it was tomorrow." She upped the wattage on her smile and Trey look relieved.

"So tonight's okay?"

"Yep. Seven-thirty at the Regal. I'll meet you there. I have a few errands to run first."

"Sounds great. See you." He left with a buoyant step, while she felt like a tramp.

She knew she teetered on the edge of falling hard for Jack Bloom all over again, if she hadn't already. Maya had warned her to be wary, but Ann could only fight his bright blue eyes, the warmth in his kiss and the care in his touch for so long. He wanted to date her. To be a couple. It freaked her out as much as it thrilled her to be the center of his attention.

Ann hurried home. She needed privacy for the call she had to make. With Jack now working at the university fulltime, he couldn't just pop over during the day like before. She settled down, rehearsed what she wanted to say, then called him.

He answered right away. "Hey, beautiful."

She forced herself to sound calm. "Hi, Jack. How are you?"

"Better now that I'm talking to you. Hold on." His voice drifted. "No, put that in Professor Burrow's room." He came back. "Sorry. What's up?"

"I have to cancel tonight." They'd planned to grab a burger together.

"Anything wrong?"

Do or die time. Be your own woman. He doesn't own you. She took a deep breath then quietly let it out. "No. I'm going to a movie with Trey, one of my coworkers."

"Trey." He paused. "That's a guy."

"Yep."

More silence.

"He asked me last week and I said I'd go. I forgot, but he reminded me today."

"A movie. With Trey. Sounds like a date."

"We're just friends. Co-workers." She felt as if she'd done something wrong, and that annoyed her. "Look, I said I'd go with him. I can't back out now. And it's not as if you and I are dating."

"So it's a no then?"

"What?"

"I asked you to be mine. As in, we date each other and *only* each other. You said you'd think about it."

She bit her lip, unsure if she'd done the wrong thing or the right thing by keeping Trey's date. "I'm still thinking."

He didn't sound upset. Just the opposite. Jack sounded too polite, too understanding. When they'd been kids, he'd yelled when angry. This calm, rational approach to conflict unnerved her. She preferred the yelling because it seemed more honest.

"So tonight is off. Okay."

"Okay?"

"Yeah. I'd like us to go to dinner on Thursday though. Remember? With my family? Will that work?"

Relieved he wasn't angry, she immediately agreed. "Sure, that's fine." *Damn it.* Why did his approval matter so much? *Why? Because you like him more than you should, you stupid woman,* her inner Maya replied.

"Great. I'll tell my parents we'll see them then. Bye." He disconnected before she could sputter more questions.

Dinner with a guy who wanted to deepen a relationship… with his *parents*? Nothing but trouble. What was her life coming to?

She sighed, then ran the errands she'd mentioned to Trey before meeting him at the movies.

To her relief, they had a great time. Trey didn't pressure her for anything afterward, just some ice cream at the Ben & Jerry's next door, and she'd learned more about a colleague with a great sense of humor. He didn't even try to kiss her, thank God. Toward the end, they'd agreed the night had been fun, but a relationship at work might be too weird. She left with a smile on her face and returned home...only to find Jack waiting for her on her porch.

Nerves flared. She parked the car and composed herself. She stopped to greet him on the porch. "Hello."

"Hey." He kissed her, a nice appreciative peck that eased her nerves. He didn't appear upset. "Good movie?"

"Dramatic, but fun. Trey's a nice guy." She let Jack inside with her since he seemed to be behaving himself and told him all about Trey. In the kitchen, she grabbed herself a bottle of water and turned to him. "Want some—"

"Yeah." Before she could blink he had her up on the counter, his mouth on hers, his hands everywhere.

She couldn't think as he drew her into his wicked web of lust, need and damn it, love. The urgency of the kiss and the pleasure he evoked by taking charge had her mindless, on the edge.

He cupped her between her legs and ground his palm against her clit. His roughness excited her, and she came, her cry of relief swallowed by his kiss. He calmed her with more kisses, stroking her legs, her waist, her shoulders.

His eyes were bright with passion and more than a hint of anger. But he only smiled and backed away. "See you tomorrow."

The bastard left her sitting on her kitchen counter, dumbfounded and wondering what the hell had just happened.

And why she wanted it to happen again.

• • •

Jack couldn't see straight as he took a frustrated walk around the block before heading back to Dan's. He swore with every step, unable to believe the obtuse woman didn't seem to have a problem going out to the movies with some fuckhead teacher. From all she'd described, the guy seemed harmless. Hell, she'd come right home from the post-movie ice cream and even wore a drop of vanilla bean on her jacket. He had no reason to disbelieve her. But knowing she'd been out with someone else when he'd staked his claim bothered the shit out of him.

Hopefully his performance in the kitchen had reminded her where she belonged. He hadn't missed how she'd succumbed to his kiss. Hell, she hadn't made a single argument about finding him waiting for her.

That helped ease his fury, but not by much. Because getting her off excited him, and now he had to deal with being sexually frustrated in addition to the idea that his girlfriend had yet to commit.

Tomorrow night would be interesting, to say the least. He was rather proud of luring her to dinner with his family. If that didn't spark a commitment, with his mother in fine form, he didn't know what would. Laura Bloom might badger him, but she could be one smooth piece of work. She'd always liked Ann, Ann had loved her, and everyone liked Dan and Julie. Time to rally the team for a full court press on one stubborn school teacher.

That in mind, he headed home—to Dan's home. Time to take care of his own living situation.

The next day, he continued to familiarize himself with the campus and adjust to his schedule. Arriving in the middle of the semester had worked in his favor, allowing him time to discuss the course structure with the department head, observe his fellow academics, and rewrite the proposed syllabus for his advanced classes. In January he'd start teaching, but for now he had time during the day for research and to get things done.

Like sign rental papers.

After returning to the house, he made a mental timeline. He still had a few days to gather his things, then he planned to move into his new place. But tonight he intended to concentrate on his complicated relationship with Ann.

"Yo, little bro." Dan peeked his head into the kitchen, on a work break, apparently. The couple's home office gave them enough space to work together when necessary, though Julie normally went in to St. Charles to teach at the hospital's computer lab while Dan telecommuted.

"Big bro." Over the years, the pair had fought as only brothers could, but he loved Dan and would do anything for him. Knowing his brother still looked out for him came as no surprise. The Blooms had raised fine sons, as his mother liked to remind him.

"How's it going with Ann?"

"Okay I guess." He threaded his fingers through his hair. "No, not really. She went out with some douchebag last night. But it wasn't a date, according to her, just a movie."

Dan winced. "Ouch."

"Not a date my ass. She's testing me. She hasn't said yes or no to being exclusive, so I'm not supposed to be mad about her movie night. Yeah, right."

"So what happened last night? You went to her place, didn't you?"

"Yes. I was nice. Polite. Asked about the movie. Then, well, I left her happy as hell while I walked off a bad case of blueballs."

Dan gave him a high five. "Good man. There you go. Then what?"

"Then I came home before I forgot myself and stayed the night. Which probably would have sent her on a date with someone else to prove some fucked up point." And why was that? He'd sensed her attraction, even her affection. He hadn't imagined the tenderness in her eyes when she looked at him, had he?

"You sure you know what you're doing with Ann? Last time you guys dated, she broke your heart."

He'd never told his family about Ann stepping out with Terry, just that they'd broken up. But damn, that still enraged him. She should have talked to him if he hadn't been the man she'd needed him to be.

"Jack?"

"What?"

"Relationships aren't easy."

"No shit, Sherlock."

Dan smacked him upside the head. "Idiot. Listen to me. I know it seems like Julie and I have no problems, but we started off rocky. She was dating some jock with balls bigger than his brains, so I had to show her that geeks are hot too."

Jack snorted. "You? A geek? You were captain of your college soccer team."

"And a computer science major, don't forget. Her ex was the starting quarterback and a bigger prick I've yet to meet." Dan huffed. "Took a while, but I wore her down. She didn't know what hit her when I pulled out the big guns. That's right. The Bloom charm."

"God. Stop helping." Like their father had with their mother, Dan had worn Julie down with persistence. She'd called him her sweet stalker and had said yes to put him—and her—out of their misery.

Dan locked a meaty arm around Jack's neck. "Don't

worry. I'm here for you. Want to have some fun and go thump the movie guy?"

"I would, but I get the sense he was just an excuse to see if I'd go all caveman on her. Ann acts like she wants to be with me, but I think the past is always there hanging between us. It shouldn't be, but sometimes I feel it too."

"So deal with it and get it done. You know women like to talk."

"Talking isn't my bag."

"Make it your bag. We're Blooms, son. Smarter than the average schmoe."

"True." Jack frowned. "It's just...I hate to go back there. It wasn't a good scene during senior year. Hell, we were both just kids."

"She's a smart girl. She'll understand that, right? She made mistakes. You made mistakes. Get some closure and get over it already. Then step up and nab the woman. Jesus, act like you have a pair."

"Pair of what?" Julie asked, startling them both.

"Oh, ah, hey baby. Didn't hear you come in."

"Probably because you were too busy beating your chest," she said drily. "Jack, you want my opinion—"

"He doesn't," Dan said.

"I do," Jack said, ignoring his brother's scowl.

"Then be honest with her. And yes, talk. You can't let go of the past until you let go of the past. Get it?"

"She's so smart." Dan gushed, a little too condescendingly because Julie narrowed her eyes and shot him an obscene gesture. He grinned. "Maybe later, baby."

She huffed and went back to her office.

Dan chuckled. "She's gonna make me pay later. Whoo-ee."

"Gross. Stop using me to spark your pathetic love life."

"At least I have one I can count on. Take Julie's advice

and try not to blow it at dinner."

Try not to blow it. Stellar advice. Now how to make sure he didn't do anything stupid to scare her off. Like go back over there and demand she go through her date that wasn't a date, minute by minute.

Chapter Fourteen

Ann arrived at Dan and Julie's, burying her butterflies under a bright smile. She refused to be intimidated by Jack's family. She'd once had a terrific relationship with them after all, and Julie seemed genuinely nice.

Jack kept it cool but friendly, and she was thankful he didn't act as if they were any closer than they were. His possessiveness last night had left her breathless and more than satisfied. Had she been Maya, she would have crowed her success in getting the man to lose his cool. Tonight would be the perfect opportunity to dismiss him in front of his family, but in such a nice way she'd come across as a kind young woman while crushing him in the process.

Alas, she wasn't Maya. She secretly adored the fact he'd been jealous about Trey but in control of himself enough not to let it all show. And making her come like that, being so forceful and demanding, still gave her shivers when she thought about it.

She'd come to the conclusion that she no longer needed revenge to get closure—she needed to know *why* it had all happened the way it had. Then maybe they could move on, become the couple he seemed to want. Having dinner with his family seemed the right way to go about it.

"Josh is thrilled to have his teacher over for dinner," Julie confided as she and Dan moved around the kitchen. Jack had set the table and talked with his mother in the dining room while his father kept an eye on said second-grader.

"I'm excited to be here. I hate cooking, and the company seems ideal. A win-win."

Julie grinned. She and Dan made a handsome couple. Ann wondered if Jack and she would have been as happy today if they had stayed together all those years ago. Would they be married with children, divorced and hating each other or broken up before they'd ever said "I do"?

"Deep thoughts?" Jack asked as he rejoined her.

"Wondering if I can get myself invited somewhere else tomorrow night," she teased, unnerved with thoughts of permanence. "So I don't have to cook again. That smells terrific, Julie."

The party moved to the table, and during dinner she laughed as much as she ate. Sam and Laura had a wonderful way of playing off each other, and their loving relationship gave the meal a lighthearted feel.

"I'm going to tell everybody you came to *my* house for dinner," Josh bragged.

"How about you just tell Heath? Not everyone needs to know our business," Julie cautioned. "Besides, you don't want all the other kids to be jealous."

"Yes I do."

Everyone laughed at that.

"He gets his chattiness from you, you know," Sam said to his wife.

Jack nudged Ann. "True."

Dan nodded. "Yeah, Mom."

Laura flushed and snapped at her husband, who laughed it off. Then Julie stood up for Laura and invited Ann's opinion on the subject.

"I can't say much. I'm just a guest."

"Oh, poo on that," Laura said.

Josh looked delighted. "Ha! Poo!"

Dan and Jack groaned, and Ann choked on a laugh.

"You know me, Ann. I'm the same woman I was when you and Jack were dating in high school."

The brief silence could have turned awkward, but Jack covered smoothly. "In that case, you probably don't want Ann defending you, Ma."

"Nonsense. I'm not one to spread rumors."

"From what I remember, you were everyone's favorite parent," Ann said with a smile. "Whenever we had a party, the class wanted you to chaperone."

"See?" Laura preened.

Ann continued, "And wasn't it Dan who got caught passing notes and being chatty in school?"

"Ah ha! I knew it." Julie gloated. "You *were* a troublemaker back then."

Dan redirected the blame. "Me? No way. Try Jack."

Instead of engaging, Jack subtly turned the conversation to Dan and Julie's new addition. Ann loved how excited Josh seemed at the prospect of a brother or sister.

An odd longing struck her. Perhaps being around such a happy home made a difference, but since seeing Jack again, old wants returned with stinging clarity. She'd always figured they'd marry and have two kids, a boy and a girl. Now she was in a position to financially support children, with a home and a job she loved, and she felt…incomplete.

Jack wanted to date her, but they had a lot of unfinished business. She was nearly thirty, not getting any younger, and had no prospects on the horizon for a husband. Even if Jack wanted to date her, she feared he'd bolt at thoughts of diapers and playdates.

His arm crept around her shoulders, and she tensed. He hadn't been very touchy in front of his family, so she'd taken her cues from him. Granted, she was still deciding how to go about dealing with him—as a boyfriend or just friends with benefits—but he'd been standoffish since she'd arrived. Now a visible hug?

His parents saw but ignored the gesture as Laura harangued her husband. Dan raised a brow and Julie grinned, but otherwise no one said a word. Josh seemed too focused on avoiding his broccoli to care about what his uncle did with his teacher.

Then Jack leaned closer and whispered, "How about we bolt after dessert? My mother only has so much patience before she'll start trying to size you up for a wedding dress."

She'd been sipping her wine when he spoke and choked when it went down wrong. Wedding dress?

She could see him trying not to laugh as he patted her back.

"Jack, don't break the girl's spine. Give her some water," Laura suggested.

"Yes, Ma."

Laura slid Josh's plate closer to him and pointed at his broccoli. "And you, eat."

"Grandma's bossy," the boy muttered.

Julie sighed. "No, she's a mom. This is what happens when you have boys. You sound bossy because they don't listen. Now eat your trees."

He forked one and ate it, making the most god-awful faces. Even Ann felt bad for him as she sipped her water.

Jack leaned close to her and said in a low voice, "Five bucks says he spits it out in his napkin and hides it under the table."

She watched the boy do just that and nearly choked again on laughter.

The meal wrapped up, dessert and coffee followed, and Ann left with Jack, thanking everyone for a lovely time.

"I don't think I've ever laughed so much or had such fun watching a child hide broccoli before." In the corner, Josh sulked. "Thanks for having me."

She got hugs and kisses goodbye, a more than friendly greeting she hadn't expected, yet the inclusion felt wonderful. Even Josh took time out from his punishment to hug her goodbye.

Walking with Jack back to her house, they didn't speak, enjoying the crisp night air. His hand grasped hers and held on, and they continued in companionable silence.

Once on her porch, he stopped her. "Can I come in?"

"I think it's time we talked, don't you?"

His smile took her off balance. He hadn't seemed to want to discuss the past before. Or had she been wrong? "Sure. I have a few things to tell you."

Once inside though, he kissed her before she could speak. When they parted, they were both breathing hard.

"God. I've been wanting to do that all night."

"Me too," Ann admitted on a sigh and stroked his cheek. "I thought you were still mad at me though."

"Mad? Why? Because you went out on a date with some dickhead teacher—a guy you see every day—when *we're* an item?"

"We're not an item…yet." She didn't sound convincing, even to herself. His smug grin made her want to slap him. Then hug him.

"I rented a house today."

She lost all train of thought. "What?"

"Yeah. That cute blue house on Shield? The one with the big tree in front? I'm renting it for a few months until I figure out where I'm moving."

"Oh." She tried to digest that.

"With Dan and Julie back, I know they need their own space. Besides, living with my slob of a brother is more than I can handle."

She smiled. "That bad, huh?"

"If you think dirty socks are gross, they're just the tip of the iceberg. I've tripped on more shoes, seen more dirty underwear, wet towels on the floor, and—"

She interrupted his tirade with another kiss. This one she led, and she showed him how much she cared without saying a word. This way she wouldn't have to put herself on the line and risk rejection by admitting how she felt out loud.

Jack slowly took over the embrace until she clung to him. "Angel, I want you. Right now. Just you and me and your bed."

She walked back with him to the bedroom, dropping clothes as they went. They moved onto her bed, bared to each other and entwined. He thrust inside her, moving faster and deeper while she held on and enjoyed being the center of his world. Jack could make her feel so special and precious at times like this. He kissed her, touched her, watched her and never broke eye contact as he made love to her. Each thrust seemed to go deeper, as if he were melding into her.

Sappy, and far too much emotion to handle as he continued to lead her into an orgasm which shattered her. He came moments after she did—no condom, just him and her, naked and exposed.

Since their bet last Friday, something had changed between them. It wasn't just about having sex without protection. Or the lack of inhibitions between them. Ann felt closer to him than she ever had before. It scared her, because she couldn't bring herself to commit to a relationship.

She'd gone and been stupid, she admitted. She was falling

for him all over again. Bad enough he rocked her world, but his generosity of spirit and love for his family rounded out the ideal partner she'd always wanted. Then to see his little neatness quirks, his irritation with his brother and jealousy with her "date" showed the very human side of him. A flawless man, no matter how handsome, would bore her. Jack was far from perfect, but he was also the only one she imagined by her side when she thought about the future.

Catching her breath while he kissed her and finished inside her, she watched him, committing each gesture and touch to memory.

"You're so sweet," he said and rolled them to their sides, hugging her. He remained inside her, softening, yet still connected. "I don't want to leave you."

"Don't yet." *Don't ever.* "Just lay with me."

He kissed her and smiled against her lips. "Now that's one order from a bossy lady I'll take."

She tried not to laugh. "I'm not bossy. That's your mother. You don't have us confused, do you?"

"I just had incredible, mind-blowing sex with you. Never mention my M-O-M in conjunction with my cock, okay?"

"Now I'm grossed out."

He chuckled and hugged her. "Close your eyes and relax. Trust me, I have a lot more to share with you."

But when she next woke, the alarm clock read three a.m. She was on her side, Jack behind her with a thick arm over her. His warm breath brushed her neck, and she felt safe. Loved.

Panicked.

She shifted.

"Ann?" he hugged her tighter but didn't sound fully awake.

"Jack?"

He gave a satisfied grunt, kissed her neck and continued

to hold her.

Despite her worry, she didn't want him to go. She extricated herself enough to set her alarm, then snuggled back into his embrace. She'd face any recriminations tomorrow. Tonight, he was hers.

The next thing she knew, a slap on her bare ass woke her.

"Up and at 'em, Ms. Weaver. It's seven-thirty. You sleep like the dead, you know that?" Jack sounded way too happy this early in the morning.

She buried her head under her pillow. "I thought you hated mornings?"

He must have heard her, because he laughed. Then a firm hand spread her thighs wide. When she tried to roll off her stomach to see him, he kept her pinned down.

"No. Stay right there." In seconds, he blanketed her with his body.

"Jack?"

"I don't want to make you late for school," he said as he settled a firm erection between her legs. "But I can't stop myself. It's all your fault." He pushed himself inside her.

Still slick from last night and aroused from the feel of him, she lay trembling while he took her with long, slow strokes.

"Faster," she prodded.

"Touch yourself. Yeah."

She slid her hand down her body and fingered herself while he plowed into her with greater urgency.

"Come on, angel. Come with me. Together."

He was so much bigger than her, so strong. But he never tried to seek pleasure without ensuring she had hers first. His generosity and care touched her in places she'd thought unreachable.

"Fuck me back, Ann," he whispered as he ground into her.

She arched her ass up and plucked her clit until she came.

Just as he groaned and stiffened over her, his release hers to enjoy as well.

After he withdrew, he pulled her with him into the shower. They cleaned up in silence, each watching the other. He continued to smile at her, his grin soft and loving while she stared at him with bemusement, wondering where they went from here.

He'd stayed the night. Again. And she'd loved it.

She could almost hear Maya ranting. *Not a great way to maintain emotional distance, dumbass.*

But his entire being radiated happiness, and she found it infectious.

They dressed, him in the same clothes from last night, and met in the kitchen over a fresh pot of coffee.

He inhaled the aroma and sighed. "Coffee." He took a few sips, then smiled at her. "Because you made me *super* happy this morning, I won't insist you drive me home."

She hadn't thought about what others might think about him being gone all night. "Oh wow. That's going to be embarrassing."

"What?"

"Your brother and Julie will know you didn't spend the night there. They'll assume you went home with me."

"I did." He looked like he'd just won the lottery.

"You know what I mean." And then… "Oh no. Josh will know. He'll tell the other kids at school that I'm shacking up with his uncle."

"Really, Ann? Shacking up? Just what are you teaching my nephew?"

"It's not funny. Stop laughing."

"You want to hear something really funny? Ask me to show you my Grand Canyon."

She tried not to laugh at that and failed. "Oh God. Stop."

The tense moment that might have been turned into a

mirth- and coffee-filled morning. Before she knew it, Jack had weaseled a promise of assistance from her and her friends to move him into his place next week.

Hours later, she ate her lunch with her coworkers, wondering how the man had slipped under her defenses. "Bonnie, am I too nice?"

Her friend immediately nodded.

"Really?"

Amy Stuart, another second grade teacher, agreed. "Nothing wrong with being nice, Ann. We need more kindness in the world."

"But am I doormat?"

Amy frowned. "Not at all. Why? Has someone been bothering you?"

"No, just something I worry about. I don't want to be a pushover."

Bonnie smirked. "This have anything to do with that hunky guy who keeps bringing you flowers?"

Amy blinked. "Trey brought you flowers?"

"You think Trey is hunky?" Bonnie asked.

"Wait. How do you know about Trey?" Ann asked Amy.

"I heard him mention it to Paul and Mandy this morning. I hear the movie was nice."

Ann groaned at her overly-innocent expression. "I went to a movie as a *friend*. Trey is a great guy." She lowered her voice. "But there was no spark. Besides, if we did date and things got awkward, I'd still have to see him every day. Not a great idea to date a coworker. Not unless you're really sure about him."

"Or you like to live on the edge," added Amy.

"Good point." Bonnie nodded. "So, your flower guy. What's the scoop?"

She wished she knew. "He's an old friend who moved back in town. We dated a little when we were younger, and we might be—*might* be—rekindling something. I'm not sure yet." *Not sure how much longer I can keep denying I'm in love with him again. Stupid!*

All the signs were there—thinking about him at random times during the day, her heart racing when he called or texted, how she looked forward to their dates. And perhaps the most telling, as panicked as she felt about him having spent the night, more than anything she wanted to feel him there all over again. In her bed and in her life.

But what if none of it was real?

Chapter Fifteen

Ann spent the remainder of her day in a weird funk. The kids must have picked up on her mood, because she had to break up several fights and threaten the class with no Halloween party on Monday if they didn't stop the nonsense.

Fortunately, she made it to the bell without any blood being spilled, and even better, Josh showed no sign of knowing where his uncle had spent the night.

That evening she took a small break from Jack. She needed the time to convince her friends not to kill her for volunteering their help with his move. Especially since she had a feeling the Blacks would show up as well. She hadn't missed the way Dex had leered at Maya. Those two were ticking bombs likely to could go off at any time.

She arrived at Riley's bearing her usual cheese platter spruced up with a side of expensive Honeycrisp apple slices.

Maya answered the door and dragged her inside. "Her highness is making pumpkin bread. I love Halloween."

"Me too." Her favorite holiday. She still had to decorate the house, but with all the excitement and stress of having

Jack in her life again, she'd put off everything, even carving her pumpkin.

They joined Riley in the kitchen, watching her work. The woman had an economical ease of movement, multitasking and making it look easy.

"It's so annoying that she can cook like this and still mouth off while doing it," Maya complained.

Ann grinned. "I know."

"Don't hate, Maya. We can't all have my mad skills." Riley blew her a kiss, and Maya told her to do something to herself that usually required a partner or at least a rubber toy.

"Ah, I missed this. Such deep friendship." And there was the finger from Maya. "Our loving way of signing how we feel to one another."

Maya snickered. Riley nodded to the fridge. "Grab me some milk, would you?"

"I don't know, Riley," said Ann. "Are you driving anywhere tonight? You can be such a lush."

"Smartass." Riley laughed. "Now talk. Maya and I have some concerns about you and Jack Bloom."

"Some? Try a ton," Maya added. "And by the way, you can tell him I don't need any messages from Dexter Black in the future."

"Ah, okay." Ann toyed with the cheese plate in front of her, peeling off the plastic wrap, then putting it back.

"Ack. Stop it." Maya grabbed the tray away from her. "Talk, woman."

"I think I love him," she said in a rush.

"I knew it," her friends said at the same time. Riley sounded triumphant. Maya looked as if she might cry.

"I can't help it. He's amazing in bed. He calls me. He texts me sweet messages. And he's been so terrific. I had dinner with his family last night. Then he slept over, and I wanted him to be there tomorrow. And the next day."

"The kiss of death." Maya groaned. "You're toast."

"Pay up," Riley demanded of her. "Ann, falling in love is a good thing. I never thought you'd go through with that stupid revenge plan. I mean, revenge for what?"

Maya frowned. "For him dumping her for Thorpe, remember? Publically. What did he say about that, anyway?"

"Well, that's just it." Ann swallowed. "We haven't exactly talked about it yet."

Riley scowled. "Why not?"

"What's he hiding?" Maya wanted to know.

"I don't know. It's not just him. I kind of don't want to talk about it either. There are old wounds there, and we're new and having fun. Being with him makes me so happy. Do I really want to go dredge all that up?"

"Yes," Riley surprised her by saying. She would have pegged Maya as someone to indulge conflict, but not easy-going Riley. "Because as much as it's fun and games now, you won't be able to let it go. I know you, Ann. You need to know why, at least. He never mentioned why he left in all the time you guys were apart. Just get it out and let the old wound heal."

Maya nodded. "What she said. I would have said it another way, but yeah. Deal with it. Ignoring it never makes it go away. Hello? Me and my mother issues? Not going anywhere."

"I know." She groaned. "I'm just afraid of ruining this. I tried not to love him. I really did."

"Sure… Were your legs open or closed when you were trying so hard?"

Riley sputtered with laughter. "Maya."

"What? Girl got hooked on that boy's—"

"Do not say dick," Ann snarled. "I am not so hard up for sex that I'd fall for any man with more than six inches of steel."

"Oh. Steel, huh? And more than six?" Maya's eyes twinkled. "You go, Whorish Ann. You're a lot more fun than Nice Ann."

"Stop talking." Ann couldn't help it and laughed despite herself. "You get me so mad sometimes. I am not too nice."

"No, you're not," Maya shocked her by agreeing. "You need to realize that. Now stop being a wimp and talk to Jack. Or I'll get the answers for you." Her smile suggested her way would not be pretty.

"Um, yeah. About Jack…"

"What?" Riley asked, eyes focused on her dough.

"I kind of volunteered you two to help him move."

Two sets of shocked gazes bored holes into her. Then Riley eyed the sliced apple in her hand and put it back on the tray.

"*Excuse* me?" Maya glared.

"Sorry, but, well, it's important to me. I want you there, and I want you guys to be friends with the guy I love. Dex and Anson are busy—" she hoped "—so Jack needs the help. Look, it'll get him out of his brother's place. Do it for me, so I can have sex away from my nosy neighbors."

"Oh man. Why do you have to ask it like that? Of course I'll help one of my best buds get some." Maya's stringent moral code—to always help out a sister who needed to get laid.

"Perfect. He's not moving until next week anyway. So, Halloween at my place?" The girls nodded. "Great. Now let's talk about Anson's restaurant next to Riley's. How are we going to handle that problem?"

The collective "we" put their heads together and tried to come up with a solution to Riley's problem. But deep down, Ann knew she wouldn't be able to relax until she and Jack had their talk.

• • •

Jack waited on Ann's porch and looked around. She'd gone all out, spreading mounds of cobwebs, a jumping spider that had nearly given him a heart attack and some ghouls and goblins on her miniscule lawn.

The neighborhood was loaded with kids, so the streets had mobs of tiny monsters and superheroes roaming for candy from house to house.

He hurried to push the doorbell before a horde of ghosts could overtake him. He carried a dozen black roses for Ann, whom he knew would get a kick out of the gesture, and two white long-stemmed ones for her friends. When Maya opened the door dressed as a witch, he grinned, pleased he'd been right about her friends being there. "Trick or treat."

She stared at him and raised a brow. "*That's* your costume?"

He wore a dark black suit under a flowing cape and knew he looked damn good. For his boutonniere he wore a rotting red rose, and when he grinned, he sported two subtly placed fangs. "I'm the guy your mother warned you about."

"Fair enough." Maya let him in, and he found Riley inside wearing a witch costume as well. Long black dresses, pointy hats, and overdone makeup made the pair look more like sexy spell-casters than old hags. "Hey, guys, the stud Ann ordered is here."

"Great intro, Maya. Thanks." He handed her a white rose.

She gave him a glare, then softened and accepted it with a flourish. "My pleasure." She turned to greet a new batch of trick-or-treaters while Riley waved at him.

"Hey, handsome. Aren't you cute?"

"I was going for sexy and dangerous, but I'll take cute." He handed her the other white rose. She looked from her stem to the dozen black ones still in his hand and grinned.

"Oh yeah. You're *definitely* the man our mothers warned us about. Your witch is in the garage looking for extra spiders."

"O-kay." He hoped she wasn't trying to find ingredients to make a potion. Not that she needed one. He'd already fallen under her spell, and last night had only proven it to him.

He found her teetering on a ladder and rushed to steady her.

"Thanks—oh. Hi, Jack." She smiled at him, and like her friends, she made witchery look sexy.

"Are vampire-vitch relations okay with your vitch council?" he asked in a spooky accent. "Because I vant to suck your blood right now."

"Tell you what. As soon as I get those glow-in-the-dark spiders down from the top shelf, you can suck away."

"Come down from there." He yanked her over his shoulder and gently set her down. Jack handed her the flowers, then used the rickety ladder to fetch her box of spiders. "Plastic. Thank God. I thought you went native and were after the real deal."

"No, just the glowy ones. They're to put on the webs on the porch. I totally forgot about them until Joey Hindenmeier told me they were missing."

"Good old Joey." He had no idea who the kid was.

"You brought me black flowers." She blinked at them, then looked closer at the band holding them together. "Is this a ring?"

A piece of black satin tied the thorny flowers together, and attached to that he'd affixed his old high school ring. What he'd once given to Ann.

"I know this is your favorite holiday."

"You remembered how much I love black roses."

"Not hard to remember, actually. You're the only woman

I know who thinks they're cool, not creepy." He smiled but grew concerned to see her tearing up. "Ann?"

"Your ring?" She cleared her throat. "Kind of an odd present."

"Not really. It was always yours." He hadn't planned to do this in a garage of all places, but the words needed to be said, and he couldn't wait any longer. Time was not on his side with the witches in the house. Unable to hold it any longer, he blurted, "I'm yours."

"Jack?"

He kissed her, then pulled back to see her. "Honey, I'm in love with you. I have been since the first moment I laid eyes on you."

"In fifth grade?" she rasped.

"Well, the first moment I laid eyes on you after you got boobs."

She wiped a tear from her eye and snorted. "There's my Mr. Romance."

"After that first date, I knew. You were mine. It wasn't puppy love. Not a first romance or first sexual experience that made me think you were it. I just felt it, in here." He brought her hand to his heart. "We never talked about what happened back then. And you know, I just don't care anymore. Terry Chapman doesn't matter. *You* matter, Ann. I love you."

"Oh my God." Riley's voice rang out from the doorway behind them. The door slammed shut before Maya could respond.

Just the two of them again, the way it should have been in all the years since they'd been apart.

"You love me?" Ann put the flowers on a shelf and gripped his hands in hers. "I-I love you too, Jack. And it scares me to death."

His heart felt overfull. "Trust me. I know."

She opened her mouth then closed it and frowned. "Terry

Chapman? I haven't heard that name in years."

"Yeah, well, I'd rather not talk about him if it's all the same to you." He hated the thought that she'd gone to Chapman behind his back. "But fuck it. I have to know, then I promise we'll never mention him again. Why him? I mean, was I that bad in bed or something?" He felt his cheeks heat, but the not knowing killed him. If she admitted he'd been lacking, he could move on. After all, he'd learned a lot since high school.

"Wait. I'm still confused. Terry Chapman?"

"Ann, I know."

"Know what?"

He frowned. She seemed genuinely confused. "I know about you and Terry, that you slept with him."

"Are you *insane*?"

"What are you talking about? Everyone knew. Selena told me—"

"Selena?" Ann's eyes darkened. "That *bitch*."

"Hold on." The truth started to emerge. "Selena told me she'd seen you and Terry making out at the bonfire before homecoming. Tim and Darren confirmed it. Are you saying they all lied?"

"Hell yes, they all lied! Why didn't you ask me about him? I would have told you as much."

Dumbfounded, he barely noticed when she let go of his hands. "Really? You never slept with him? That's why we broke up."

"We broke up because *you* were seeing Selena on the side."

"I only went out with her because you were doing Chapman. Wait, wait." He clutched his head, his whole world turned around. "So you never cheated on me with Terry?"

"No. I didn't." She planted her hands on her hips, and dear God, he believed her.

"Holy shit." He wanted to strangle Selena then toss the remains to Ann for real retribution. "I'm so sorry. I thought…"

"But why?" Her eyes pooled, bewitching, bewildered. "I loved you so much. I was devastated when you broke up with me—for *her* of all people. You were so cruel about it."

As if it were yesterday, he remembered the scene in the school lunchroom. "Damn. I thought—"

"If you had asked me about it back then, we could have talked. We always used to tell each other everything. Why didn't you ask me?"

His face felt hot. "Because I was afraid."

"Of what?" She took his hand, and his heart raced like crazy.

He was embarrassed to admit it. "Afraid I'd driven you to him. That it was my fault. Hell, Ann. You were the only girl I'd ever been with. Sexually."

"I know." She gave him a wan smile.

"I never seemed to last that long, and the guys always talked about how to be better in bed. About how the girls measured us by how we performed."

"*I* never did that."

"I didn't think you had. But Terry had a rep for being a real stud, and everyone knew he was into you. Then Selena and a few guys kept talking about him and you. And there was a rumor you were done with me and wanted him instead. I was embarrassed. I thought I was a stud, and it turned out you thought I was a limp dick."

"I did *not*."

"God, I get it now. I was ashamed and pissed, so I thought I'd embarrass you instead. I had no idea… If I see her again, I'm going to—"

"No. Let it go." She moved into his arms and hugged him, and he felt like everything might just work out. "All this time

I never knew. I mean, we were so happy and the world was ours." She paused and quieted. "Then you threw me over. I thought you'd been cheating on me."

He pulled back to stare at her. "Ann, I never looked twice at anyone else. If I hadn't been more interested in saving my pride, I would have known you would never cheat on me."

"Certainly not with Terry Chapman." She grimaced. "He was a pig. One of Selena's throwaways, I think."

"That ass. So you never cheated. I was good in bed even back then?" His voice lilted like a question, and he wore a grin so wide he felt the joy to his toes.

"For the record, I never cheated. You were a major stud, but nowhere near as good as you are now."

"Good. You keep thinking that." He kissed her, wanting her right now.

She put a hand on his chest and ended the kiss. "And you and Selena…?"

"Are you kidding? I thought I sucked in bed. You think I wanted to sleep with her and have it confirmed? We dated in public to rub your nose in it. And no, I'm not proud I did that, but at least I never fucked her." He shivered. "Thank God."

"Well, she is on marriage number three."

"Four, actually." He shook his head. "Yep. Karma's hitting her hard. But I don't think she's noticed."

"Not as hard as Maya's going to want her hit her when she finds out what she did."

He grinned. "Those two really hated each other."

She tugged his cape. "So I get to keep you, the flowers and the ring?"

"They're all yours. The flowers are new, but the ring and I have always been yours."

They kissed, and he knew he'd never look at Halloween the same way again. There really was magic to be had under a full moon on All Hallow's Eve. Even in a musty garage.

Chapter Sixteen

Maya sneezed from the dust she'd kicked up. "I can't believe he didn't just hire someone to move him."

"Are you still bitching?" Riley sighed and carried another box into the dining room of Jack's new place. "I'm glad you guys finally got everything out in the open," she said to Ann.

"Yeah." Ann hadn't mentioned why Jack had believed Selena, but that he'd had cause to believe his guy friends who'd lied. No sense in wounding her man's pride.

The past week had been a magic all its own. They'd spent time at her place, but once he moved in to his, they planned to alternate sleeping arrangements. It helped that he lived so close—and that they lived apart. Their relationship had progressed too fast, and Ann needed time to process. Separate abodes gave them some distance, while only being a five minute walk from each other.

"Hey, where's the party?" A familiar voice asked.

Ann watched with amusement as Dex and Anson arrived in ratty jeans and sweatshirts.

"Time to move some junk," Dex said.

"Not junk. My personal treasures," Jack corrected. Items he'd had in a storage locker until now. Ann didn't think he had that much, but her friends had complained so much she'd have thought he had enough to fill a mansion, not a small cottage. As it was, the place had come fully furnished, and they moved only his clothes, books and sports equipment in.

"Great timing, guys," Maya snapped. "We're just about done with all the heavy lifting."

Dex grinned, unrepentant. "Awesome. That means pizza without having to work for it."

Anson arched an imperious brow at Riley. "Might want to watch those precious hands. Your bakery needs you. I need you." He winked. "Having you next door gives my builders a reason to keep coming back every day. Place smells good, I'll grant you that. You should expand if you want to show a profit though. I could help you with the financial planning."

Ann would have considered that an olive branch of sorts if he hadn't offered his help in such a patronizing tone. She understood why Riley loathed him.

"Should you be outside in the light, Anson?" Riley asked sweetly. "Your kind is known for turning to ash under the sun."

Maya snickered, and Dex coughed to hide a smile.

Ann and Jack exchanged a sigh. "I'll go get the linens box," she said.

"Right." Jack hotfooted it toward the garage. "I'll go, ah, do something away from them so I'm not called to the witness stand later."

She laughed. "Funny guy. Come help me in your bedroom when you're done."

He kissed her. "Be right back."

There were four more boxes in the storage van, and she grabbed the one marked *linens,* leaving the one labeled *weight equipment* for the Black cousins. While Anson and

Riley squared off and Dex watched on with glee, Maya joined her in the bedroom.

"You know, Riley's right." Maya helped her move boxes of clothes around so they had a clear path to Jack's new closet. "Anson is an ass."

"It's his tone."

"Makes me want to punch him." Maya bumped Ann with her hip. "I know I bet against you, but I'm glad for you and Jack. All in all, he seems like a good guy."

"He is." Ann smiled, so in love it hurt. "But we're going to do things right and take our time. No rush."

"Yeah. Leave the revenge to the professionals." Maya cleared her throat and lowered her voice. "So are you going to tell him about the baby?"

"I—"

"What?" Jack asked from the doorway, his face pale. "Revenge? What baby?"

"Shit." Maya looked like she'd just stepped in a pile of it. "I'm sorry. I meant—"

Ann blew out a breath. She hadn't planned on telling him about the miscarriage. Ever. What good would it do but hurt him and her all over again?

"Maya, can you give us a minute?" Ann asked.

"And some space," Jack added. "Tell the guys and Riley I'll pay you back later."

"Sure, sure." Maya darted out of the room and closed the door.

Ann and Jack watched each other while the sounds of their friends leaving reached them. After a second car departed, she sat on the bed, not sure where to start.

"Ann?" He stood, his arms crossed. Defensive, worried, upset. "Is there a baby?"

"Yes and no." She sighed. "It happened so long ago."

"So you're not pregnant now."

"No." She watched him carefully.

"Tell me. I need to know."

She understood as much as she didn't want to. "We used to be careful, remember?"

"Yeah."

"But a few times we weren't. One day I got really bad cramps. I thought I was having my period, but it turned out I wasn't. I went to a clinic and found out. You know, the one we went to for the condoms? I should have just told my mom we were having sex and gone on the pill. But I was embarrassed."

"I know." He sounded so sad.

She blinked to clear her eyes. "Well, my bleeding was heavy. Too heavy for a period. I'd had a miscarriage. The baby wasn't ever really there."

"You didn't tell me?"

"I wanted to, but then there you were at lunch with Selena Thorpe."

He blanched and sagged against a nearby wall. "Jesus Christ. That happened on the day we broke up?"

"Close enough. I'd lost the baby I hadn't realized I'd been carrying. It hurt, but not as much as you'd think. We weren't ready. I know I wasn't. It was a relief, to tell you the truth. But yeah, it was sad. I wanted to tell you the next day, but you dumped me. It was a shock."

"Shit. You thought I'd been sleeping with Selena. God, you must have hated me."

"I didn't know what had happened. It was all so confusing. The world just kind of fell apart in twenty-four hours."

He just stared at her, silent. Then in a small voice he asked, "Did your parents ever find out?"

She shook her head. "Just Riley and Maya. I needed their support. I couldn't tell you, of course. And my mom... It would have killed me to have her so disappointed in me. She loved you. Dad did too. But I mean, I was their little girl."

In a hoarse voice, he said, "I get it. I do." He stared at her, and she didn't know how to feel.

On the one hand, revealing her secrets relieved her. But on the other, she hated seeing his pain. "I'm so sorry, Jack."

"It's not your fault."

"No. And it's not yours either." She left the bed to reach out to him. She stroked his cold fingers. "It wasn't meant to be."

"I guess not."

She kissed the back of his limp hand. "Do you forgive me for not telling you?"

"Of course." He stood straighter and seemed to shake off his mood. "Talk about a revelation."

"I know. Hell of a moving day."

They shared a shaky laugh, and he cupped her cheek. "Something else Maya said."

Hell. She'd hoped he hadn't remembered that part.

"What did she mean about revenge?"

She dropped her gaze, feeling horrible for ever having thought up the plan.

"Ann?"

She moved back to gather her thoughts.

In a quiet voice, he asked, "Is that what all this is? You getting your revenge on me for the baby?"

"The baby? No. I had put that behind me. But in a way, I guess, I'd have to say yes. That's how it started." She wanted no more lies between them.

He looked away from her and clenched his hands. She wanted him to yell, not do his quiet thing where he seemed to accept what came at him without a stink.

"Jack, listen. I heard you were back in town, and I was angry. I admit that. But it had nothing to do with the miscarriage. A spontaneous abortion, the doctor called it." She thought that might sound better, a less hurtful term, but he didn't react other than to continue staring away from her.

"The girls and I had some wine and were talking smack. We learned you and Dex and Anson were back in town, three guys who'd done us wrong—or so we thought at the time. To get some closure, we decided to get back at you."

He glanced at her, and the angry pain darkening his eyes sucked her breath away. "So this—us—was about getting back at me? What? Making me fall in love with you so you could dump me the way I once dumped you?"

"No. Don't be—"

"But you just said—"

"We'd been drinking. It was a stupid idea. I was going to use and lose you. There. I said it." Ann was all about truth, but for some reason, doing the right thing and coming clean didn't seem to be helping her. "Jack, that was before I knew the real you. I told you I love you, and I meant it. The past is the past. Let it go."

"I have. I didn't care about you and Terry when I thought you'd been together. I just wanted you, Ann. But this whole time you've been plotting to date me, then break up with me?"

"No. Listen, damn it." How had everything turned sour in a matter of minutes?

"I can't... I have to go. I need to think." He gave her a wide berth and slammed out of the house. She didn't hear a car, so he had to be walking. But he'd left her. Again.

He needed time to accept what she'd told him. In his place, she supposed she'd need the same. When he settled down and remembered what they'd shared, everything they meant to each other, he'd come around. Then they could straighten out the truth from the lies and have their happily ever after.

A tear slid down her cheek.

She hoped.

• • •

Jack had never felt so lost. He didn't know what to think or how to feel. He sure as hell didn't want company though, so he walked away from the neighborhood. Two miles up the road toward the mountains, he turned onto a popular trail. Then another half mile he turned again, onto a barely used path he'd come across when he'd first arrived back in Bend.

A baby.

He couldn't wrap his mind around thoughts of his and Ann's child. The words *miscarriage* and *spontaneous abortion* didn't compute, because he kept seeing a baby in Ann's arms, one with his dark hair and her blue eyes.

He wanted to scream at the unfairness of it all. Selena Fucking Thorpe, Chapman, the guys from the football team that he'd thought were his friends. They'd all colluded to break him and Ann up. And when she'd needed him most, he hadn't been there.

"It wasn't meant to be," she'd said. He knew she had made peace with the loss, but he hadn't yet. Yes, it had been gone before it had lived. But a baby…

He walked until his thighs burned and his calves stung. The sun started to fade. He walked some more. Every so often his cell phone vibrated in his pocket.

Along his walk, he faced some hard truths.

Ann was right about the baby. They hadn't been ready, and nature must have sensed it. He felt stupid for being so attached to something so long ago, but he thought he deserved to mourn. What kind of bastard would he be to feel nothing for what might have been his child?

But the other truth, the thing that continued to haunt him and maybe always would… Had Ann really been stringing him along? He'd confessed his love, had thought she had too. Yet… She'd been icy to him that first day when he'd picked up Josh. Why date a guy she thought had not only cheated on her, but dumped her for Selena after such a traumatic experience?

That stymied him. In her place, he well understood her need for revenge. But how much of what she felt for him had been real, and how much was staged? She now knew he had been a victim to Selena's lies, like her. But what did that mean in the grand scheme of things?

They weren't moving in together. She had her place, he had his. She'd agreed to take things slowly. Did she have another motive for wanting space? So that when *she* dumped *him* this time, she had her own place to go back to?

He wished he knew what she really thought. He hated feeling stupid. Used. And he wasn't even sure he deserved to feel bad, because she could be telling the truth. Maybe she did love him after all. He hadn't been as bad as he'd thought he was in high school. He'd sexually satisfied her. He knew that much.

But the rest? Affection or revenge? Did she love him? Could she after what she'd suffered at such an impressionable age? The more he thought about it, the worse he felt. Ann had a reason to be angry, but she was at heart a kind woman. Maybe she'd started out with the intent to get him back but had lost her nerve. What if he'd been steadily falling in love, and she'd been feeling nothing but gentle affection? What if now she didn't know how to let him down easily and was going out with him out of a sense of misguided pity? Christ, that would be worse than her trying to make him pay for the past. Dating him because she was too nice to hurt his fucking feelings.

He continued to think long and hard on his way back. He texted everyone who'd called him that he was fine, just needed some time to think. To Ann, he sent the same. A generic but polite message to give him some space alone.

And he felt even hollower without her, moron that he was.

• • •

Ann didn't know what do to. It had been a week. Jack wasn't talking to her. Maya was beside herself apologizing every time they met. Ann sat on Riley's couch, trying to believe things could still work out while her friends tried to cheer her up.

"God, Ann. If I'd just kept my mouth shut I—"

"Enough! Maya, so help me, if I hear one more apology from you, I will slap you into tomorrow," Ann snarled. "He overheard the truth. Fine. The problem isn't you or him, it's me. I never should have come up with that stupid idea for revenge in the first place. It was a terrible thing to do, and it backfired on me."

"Karma," Maya said, subdued.

"Enough with the meekness. Bitch up, damn it."

Maya blinked. "Bitch up?"

"I think she means man up," Riley said. "Except you're not a man, so…"

"Oh." Maya grinned, looking relieved. "I like it."

Ann muttered, "You would. Okay, you two. I'm at the end of my rope. What do I do?"

"About?"

"Hello? *Jack*. Who the hell have I been talking about?"

"There. That's what you needed." Riley and Maya nodded.

"What? A headache from explaining myself to the thickheaded one?"

"I prefer dense," Maya said. "Kidding. No, you needed some fire under your ass. You've been trudging around like the walking wounded. Bitch up yourself. Get over it."

Before Ann could light into her, Riley put a hand on her

shoulder. "I think what Maya means is that we're worried about you. The last time you fell for Jack, it all imploded. This time the truth came out. So Jack needed his time to process. I think a week is plenty."

Maya nodded. "Me too. You need to take care of this. No more sulking for you or the sexy vampire. And yeah, I'm going to call him that from now on because he rocked that Halloween costume."

"And he gave us roses." Riley smiled.

"White roses. I love flowers."

Ann didn't mean to, but she started crying. She'd been overemotional all week and hiding it from everyone. Even her friends didn't know about her crying jags that lasted all night at the thought of losing Jack again. He was her best friend. A guy who had been everything she'd wanted twelve years ago and today. To learn she'd been wrong about him both hurt and elated her.

"Oh shit. Get the tissues." Maya literally hurtled the couch and grabbed Ann in a big fat hug. "Get it out, Ms. Weaver. I'm so sor—" she broke off when Ann growled at her. "I mean, I'm sad to know Jack is being an ass again. We should go fix that."

"Right. Because you've been *so* helpful up till now," Riley said drily. She handed Ann a tissue. "Clean up, girl, then get your battle armor on."

"Armor?"

"A slinky dress, makeup, and the sexiest shoes you have. Leave the underwear at home. It's time to hunt your man down and remind him who he belongs to."

"Me?"

"You," Riley and Maya said as one.

Then Maya gave Ann a wicked grin. "You have to set a trap, and I know just how to do it."

Chapter Seventeen

"You look like shit, Jack." Dex shook his head as the pair of them worked to straighten up Dex's back room. The studio was perfect, with the right amount of light and space to have several backdrops for portraits, as well as comfort for staged shoots and costumes.

But the back storage room needed some new shelving, and Jack needed something—anything—to take his mind off Ann. He would talk to her again soon. Just…not until he was ready. He couldn't figure out how to deal with her yet. But God, he missed her.

"Dude, you stare any harder at the shelf, it won't need nails. You can hammer it in through thought alone." Dex brought his hands together and made some weird meditation sound.

"Shut up, Black."

"It speaks! About time. How's work?"

"Okay. I enjoy helping the TAs, and I've made some great inroads on new research with solar power. I've written a syllabus the head guy likes, and I'm rewriting some course work for fun."

"For fun." Dex blinked. "You really are a nerd under that muscle, aren't you?"

"You'd know. Poin*dexter.*"

Dex held his hands over his heart and staggered. "Bastard. Hit me right where it hurts, why don't you?"

Jack shook his head, chuckling. "Where's Anson?"

"Where else? Fighting with Riley."

"He'd do better to leave her alone before she feeds him a poisoned cupcake."

Dex sighed. "Sad thing is, he'd take it in a heartbeat if she offered. He's stupid enough to eat it and die to prove a point."

"What? That he has the hots for Riley?" Jack wasn't blind. Well, not all the time. When it came to Ann, he couldn't think straight. With everyone else, he knew just how to handle them. He'd been smart enough to avoid his family with work excuses. None of them knew of his personal troubles, and he wanted to keep it that way.

Anson and Dex did, of course, and they'd been nothing but supportive. Hearing that the girls were out for vengeance put them both on the alert. Jack kept Ann's miscarriage and his other worries a secret though. Some things even best friends didn't need to know.

"You ever going to talk to her again?" Dex asked. He'd been a quiet shoulder to lean on, not bugging Jack about details, just listening. Anson had given him several strategies for dealing with her, none of which had any appeal.

"Yeah. I just don't know what to say. I mean, she had a reason to want my head on a platter."

"And you can't trust that she means it when she says she loves you."

"You know Ann. She's got a heart. She might have started the relationship with the idea to screw me over, but once she knew the truth, she'd never have gone through with it."

Dex blinked. "If you know that, then you know she won't lie about dumping you."

Jack sighed. "Yeah, but what if she went on dating me just to save me more heartache. God, I said heartache. I'm turning into a woman." He hated thinking so hard about fucking *feelings*.

Dex coughed. "Well, um, I don't think I'd say—"

"I am way over-thinking things. So we didn't work out once? Doesn't mean we can't still be friends, right? She probably feels sorry for me. And damn, but pity will kill a hard-on faster than—"

"Than what, Jack?"

He blinked at the woman who filled the doorway. It couldn't be.

"Are you fucking kidding me?" It took everything he had in him not to launch himself at Selena Thorpe and demand some serious apologies. He wanted to spank the woman, but not in a good way.

"Oh boy." Dex angled himself between Jack and the doorway. No doubt he'd seen the murder in Jack's eyes.

Selena frowned. "Are you mad at me? I came out here because someone told me you were looking for me." She smiled at him in invitation. "Heard I'm single again? I am. And, honey, you are even better looking than you were in high school. Hel-lo, handsome." She ignored Dex.

Jack said to Dex, "If she's not out of here in five seconds, woman or not, I'm going to kick her ass back to Portland."

Selena gaped like a fish.

Dex quickly walked the woman out of the back room into his studio. Jack swore he heard Maya's voice along with Dex's, but then someone else was at the door, and he lost his ability to speak.

Ann closed and locked the door behind her. She wore the blue dress he'd bought her. It clung to her figure, leaving no question to the fact she wasn't wearing a bra. Her legs looked impossibly long, especially in those heels that added a few inches to her.

Her long wine-red hair curled around her shoulders and kissed her breasts. Jesus, she was breathtaking.

"Hello, Jack." Her smoky voice matched her smoky eyes. Her makeup was heavier, richer, and made her look like a siren out to tempt a man.

He had to clear his throat to answer her. "Ann."

She sauntered—no other word for it—toward him. He didn't know where to look. Her slender thighs, full breasts, that mouth glistening with a slick shine? Her eyes narrowed in concentration as she stalked him like the predator he believed her to be.

"What the fuck. *Ann?*"

He backed up until she pushed him down into the folding chair behind him.

"I've given you time." She put her hands on his shoulders and straddled him on the chair. "I've given you space." She squirmed over his erection, so he knew she felt him hard and hot beneath her. "But enough is enough."

He didn't understand. A ruckus outside drew his attention, as did the sound of a woman's scream. "We—"

Ann cut him off with a brutal kiss. She brought his hands up to cup her breasts, and he gave in to his desire. An entire week without her, harder to bear because he couldn't be sure if he was looking at more than a week, maybe an eternity.

She sucked on his tongue and moaned as she ground over him. He kneaded her breasts, wanting to taste more of her. She ran her lips over his cheek to his ear, kissing along the way. "I'm not wearing any panties," she whispered.

"My five favorite words." So naughty, his angel. But she didn't look all that angelic. Nor did she feel ethereal in his arms.

"Fuck me, Jack. Put that big fat cock inside me."

Caught in lust and love without reason, he had to obey. She moved back, stood and raised her dress. Nothing but a smooth, bare pussy.

He gripped her hips and shoved his face between her legs. He licked her, loving her with his tongue while he freed himself from his jeans and underwear. Then she was over him, taking him inside her and riding him as if she couldn't wait.

"Ann. Fuck. Come, baby. All over me."

"Jack. I love you." She kissed him and gripped him tight inside her, the pressure too much to bear.

It had been too long and he wanted her too much. He came hard, the jet of ecstasy rushing through him as he spent inside the woman he loved. She moaned his name, planting kisses on his lips, his cheeks, his neck. Trembling over him, she sat in silence and caressed his scalp.

When he could function again, he blew out a breath. "Ann, I—"

She slapped a hand over his mouth. "No more. We love each other. The past is done. Gone. We're over it. Say it with me." She lifted her hand.

"Ann, I don't—"

She muffled him again. The mean glint in her gaze enthralled him, because she looked honestly enraged. His angel was *pissed off.* "I said *it's over.* Deep down it was never about revenge. What I really wanted was closure. I couldn't have you, so I'd settle for getting you out of my system for good. Except you wouldn't go. From the first, I was hooked. You blew my mind. You charmed me into forgiving and forgetting. And then to learn you've always been the boy I fell in love with…" She pulled her hand away again and kissed him.

Damn if he didn't start to get hard all over again. He

broke the kiss, panting. "Are you sure? Really sure?"

"I love you, you bonehead." She smacked him in the chest, but when she shifted and felt him inside her, her eyes widened. "Are you still hard?"

"Oh yeah," he growled and rocked her over him. "Ride me. I need to come again."

They watched each other as they made love. He was lost to her. He knew it and accepted it. She owned him, body, heart and soul.

When he couldn't wait any longer, he forced her to move faster. The bumping and grinding grew into moans and a hoarse shout as he came, not caring about the mess.

"Fuck. Oh fuck." He buried his face between her breasts. Nudging her dress aside, he took a nipple in his mouth and sucked, rolling the bud while he finished inside her.

"Jack. God." She pulled his mouth away from her to kiss him again. "Quit avoiding me, okay? I love you. I want to marry you and have babies with you. I'll wait as long as I have to, but you have to forget what was, okay? For me."

He looking into her eyes and saw his future. "You really mean it?"

"I do."

A lifetime of arguments, makeup sex and joy were all bundled into his angel, into his heart. "Just promise to say those two little words when it matters and it's a deal."

Her eyes brightened. "Sucker. I finally have my revenge, Jack. You're in my clutches for all eternity." She gave a dark laugh, and he chuckled with her.

"You make the best witch ever." He shifted and started to slide out of her. "Or maybe the best devil. I swear, you could tempt me to do just about anything." He kissed her again, then froze and pulled back. "Hold on. Selena Thorpe? What the hell was that? Why is she here?"

Ann smiled and kissed him until he calmed down,

content to hold her. "Maya decided we needed some closure with her too. Selena was in town, believe it or not, visiting family. A phone call about a rich, desperate man—that would be you—asking for her had her hustling down here."

"Rich? That's a laugh. But how did you know I'd be here?"

"Dex might have helped a little too. But Selena's not important anymore. What's important is right here."

"Oh yeah. Right here in my arms. You're my world, angel."

"And you're mine. We'll leave all the scary stuff out there with the mean people." He didn't understand her sly grin, but then he didn't care because she started whispering of all the ways she planned to make up for their lost week.

"You know what they say the best revenge is?" he asked, feeling lazy, sated, and so in love he wanted to burst.

"Living well?"

"See? Great minds think alike." He pursed his lips for another kiss, and his angel didn't disappoint.

• • •

Maya stepped into Dex's studio on a mission. Oh, it burned to have to turn to him for help, but she'd seriously stepped in some heavy shit by being such a blabbermouth and needed to make amends. She wanted to smack herself for not being more careful, but with the cat out of the bag, she had no one to blame but Maya Werner, loudmouth extraordinaire.

Watching Selena Thorpe—she'd never changed her name during any of her marriages, go figure—wrap her ringless hand around Dex's thick biceps as they spoke annoyed the crap out of Maya. She didn't want Dex, but that didn't mean she wanted that blonde bitch touching anything in *her* town. Period.

Since Dex was a friend of Jack's, and Jack belonged to Ann, that meant by extension Dex was off limits.

Maya smiled, shut the studio door behind her, and walked to the couple now in deep discussion. "Selena, you whore. *Great* to see you." Maya had insisted Selena be part of the plan. It was all about wrapping things up, after all. "How've you been?"

Selena glanced over, shocked, and then narrowed her eyes. "Speaking of whores... Dexter, you let just anyone in here?"

Dex's amusement didn't matter. His studio, his presence, none of it registered as Maya focused on her target. God, she'd been waiting for this.

"Oh shit," he muttered, realizing too late she had something planned. "Maya, maybe you should—"

"Catch up with an old—and I do mean *old*—friend? Sure, Dex. Good idea."

He reached out a hand, to stop her no doubt. She grabbed it and heard him thank the Lord. Then she yanked him off balance. Not an easy feat considering the guy outweighed her by at least a hundred pounds of pure muscle.

Once past him, she didn't hesitate. She took one good look at the bitch who'd nearly ruined her friend's life—and punched.

Selena's cry of pain and the *crack* that echoed felt *so* good. Orgasmic-ly good. So she cocked her arm back to let another punch fly when a pair of arms grabbed her and dragged her away.

"Tell me you did not just cold-cock Selena," said Dex.

She struggled in his arms, trying to ignore how right he felt wrapped around her. When was the last time a guy had been able to lift her up off her feet, anyway? "Get off. I'm not done."

"Oh, I think you are," another voice said.

Shit. Anson Black, the big know-it-all, had shown up.

"I'll sue, you bitch," Selena screeched. "For everything you're worth." She bled like a stuck pig and clutched the handkerchief Anson handed her to her face. Her eyes started to swell too. "I'll hire so many lawyers your head will spin." She might have sounded a lot scarier if she hadn't been muffled behind a bloody hanky.

Maya grinned. "Fuck you. Nice raccoon eyes you got there."

Selena took a furious step in her direction. Maya tried to jerk free of Dex's hold, but the bastard couldn't be budged.

Anson stepped between them. Selena turned to him and cried, "You saw what she did. You're a witness."

"Unfortunately, I just got here. I didn't see a thing. What happened?" he asked.

Maya laughed. "I'll tell you what happened. I—"

Dex squeezed tight, and she wheezed.

"Poor Selena ran into a door. You okay, sweetheart?" Dex asked.

Anson raised a brow. "A door?"

"With squeaky hinges," he added and squeezed Maya tighter when she tried to talk.

"Gotcha." Anson hustled Selena out of the studio with the promise of a hospital visit.

Dex lessened his grip on her but hadn't set her down yet. Extraordinary strength for a guy she used to tower over.

"Um, she's gone," said Maya.

"Yep."

She wriggled and swallowed hard when she noted the sheer strength in the man's forearms. And that chest. Every breath he took emphasized the breadth of him. "Dex, you can let me go now."

"Not yet." He set her back on her feet but continued to hold her. He leaned in close to whisper in her ear, "Selena's got you by the balls you surprisingly don't have."

She froze. "Huh?"

"As usual, you leapt forward without thinking things through. You don't get divorced four times without knowing how to play the courts or who the best lawyers are. She sues you—and rightfully she could—or presses charges, and your ass is in jail and you'll be broke before she can sleep with your attorney. A slam dunk, and you lose big."

Shit. She hadn't been thinking about repercussions when she'd busted the bitch's nose. Maya knew she had anger issues, but this trumped all levels of stupidity. She felt scared for herself in a way she hadn't been in years.

"But I can make that all go away."

"How?" Was he going to offer to kill the woman? She'd asked around. Dex had been in the military. Maybe special forces. "Do you have a gun? A knife, maybe? Her brake lines could use some tampering."

"Have a— Brake lines? Are you fucking nuts?"

So not offering to kill Selena then. "Bummer."

"You are one scary woman." He chuckled. "No, I'm not going to kill her. Though I understand the impulse. That is one unpleasant woman."

"You think? Hey, can you let me go now?"

"Not yet." He rubbed his cheek against hers, and the scent of pine and man made her lightheaded. When the hell had Dex started to smell good?

"Dex…"

"See, here's the thing. Selena has her version of events, and we have ours."

"Ours?"

"You saw her bump into a door, didn't you? Because that's what I'll say if I have to."

She let that sink in. "You'd lie for me?"

"Maybe." Pause. "For a price."

"Damn it." She tried to escape him and found herself spun and pressed none too gently against the wall. The breath knocked out of her, she blinked into Dex's smoky gray eyes. "Nice way to treat a woman."

"More like a wildcat." He grinned. "Oh come on. You hit Selena a hell of a lot harder than I set you against this bulkhead."

"The what?"

"The wall, Little Miss Civilian." He winked, and she started to smile. Then, remembering exactly who was holding her prisoner, she scowled again.

He sighed. "Even sexier when you turn all mean. Okay. Let's put our cards on the table."

"Let's, you bully. What do you want?"

His grin unnerved her, because there was something wild, sexy, and a bit cruel about it. "What did I want twelve years ago? A date, Maya."

"*What?*"

"Yeah. You want to avoid jail time. I want you. You owe me…hmm…let's say ten dates. Ten romantic evenings, and we're even."

"I'm not sleeping with you to avoid going to jail!" Kinky, but even for Maya that was taking things a little too far.

He tsked. "Who said anything about sleeping? Or sex," he tacked on before she could argue semantics. "You agree to go out with me. We have fun, enjoy each other's company, but nothing you couldn't share with friends. Dinner, a movie, a walk in the park. *My* choice. But you have to try to have fun."

"Are you fucking serious?" Looking like Dex did, he couldn't have been hard up for women. He was crazy hot. Then again, if he got his dates this way, perhaps the crazy was literal.

"As a heart attack." He smiled at her, and her heart started racing away.

"So you want to go out with me. Ten times. No sex."

"Well, I won't say no to sex if you ask nicely."

She glared at him, and he laughed again.

"Ten dates and you don't rat me out for belting Selena," she said slowly. "Is that right?"

"Yes, it is," he responded just as slowly. "Has anyone ever told you that you have the most beautiful face? I mean, I could drown in your eyes."

She blushed, not sure how to handle him. Back in high school, she'd been confident. He'd been nerdy but cute. A really nice kid, except for him blackmailing her with an incriminating photograph. At the prom he'd forced her to go to, he'd surprised her by being fun too. Cute and fun. Not sexy. Not seriously hot. Not ripped like a motherfucker.

She swallowed hard and stared at the muscles of his chest, visible through his tight T-shirt.

"Well?" He moved closer, his breath whispering over her lips.

The word "Fine," whooshed out of her just as he kissed her.

And holy mother of God, but she forgot how to breathe while he seduced her into giving some tongue before he ended the kiss.

Masterful, effortless and he had her panting and leaning in for more.

It didn't help that his smirk turned her on, or that his gray eyes now seemed ink-black.

Danger stared at her from a face too captivating to belong to the old geeky Dexter Black.

"Who *are* you?"

His grin made her feel hunted. "Me? I'm your boyfriend for the foreseeable future, sweetheart. Now let's go find Anson to witness our deal, hmm?"

"Th-the kiss wasn't enough?" She needed to wash her

panties, stat.

"Good, hmm?" He laughed and dragged her with him out the front door. "Don't worry about Jack and Ann. They'll be fine. You need to start worrying about yourself, princess." He had to adjust himself as he walked, and of course she noticed that he was huge *all* over. A walking billboard for sex, and she was starving for him—*it*. Hell.

Not good. Not good at all if she wanted to get out of this stupid deal without jumping the man. Her enemy. The only person who'd ever managed to best her. She had to hold onto her mad, her passion, her—

He nipped her ear and startled a small shriek out of her. "You're not the only one who's out for revenge."

About the Author

Caffeine addict, boy referee, and romance aficionado, NY Times and *USA Today* bestselling author Marie Harte has over 100 books published with more constantly on the way. She's a confessed bibliophile and devotee of action movies. Whether hiking in Central Oregon, biking around town, or hanging at the local tea shop, she's constantly plotting to give everyone a happily ever after. Visit http://marieharte.com and fall in love.

You can contact her at marie_harte@yahoo.com.

Enjoy the entire **Best Revenge** *series...*

SERVED COLD

SERVED HOT

SERVED SWEET

Falling for the Bad Girl
a *Cutting Loose* novel by Nina Croft

Detective Nathan Carter is a cop, through and through. But his work ethic—and libido—are thrown off balance when he heads up the case against jewel thief, Regan Malloy. Because with one sizzling look, she's had him hot and hard ever since. But now Regan's out of prison and hoping to start over. It's inevitable that they'll meet up again—in bars, hotels…and hotel beds. Still, it's just desire. If they give it enough time, it'll burn itself out. Because a good boy and a bad girl can't possibly make it work. Or can they?

Shocking the Medic
a *Pulse* novel by Elizabeth Otto

Paramedic Luke Almeda can't believe he's working with his best friend, Greer. She was supposed to go off and be a hot shot lawyer like the rest of her family. He has to keep reminding himself that no matter how beautiful, sweet and caring she is, there can never be more than friendship between them. Even if it weren't prohibited at work, they are from two different worlds. And being together means they lose everything.

CPSIA information can be obtained
at www.ICGtesting.com
Printed in the USA
LVHW041033040623
748842LV00024B/200

9 781979 374750